Golden Blade, Silver Veins
by Magnus October

Edited by @rayfinnwrites
Cover art by rye fawn @ www.ryefawn.com

Chapter 1

CURSE

If ever a curse had been wrought unto the world, the immolation of Beyhar had acted as the catalyst. A power welled, vast and burning in a young elven child, and she was engulfed by it on the day of the fire. Her dark eyes danced with light as she watched flames lick at the walls of her home, the blood and flesh all around her sizzling with the heat. The girl's mother and father were no more than remnants, pieces scattered inside the cottage and onto her clothes and skin. She walked out the door, and her body was numb as she turned to watch. The girl did not need to see the magic from her hands to know it would be spreading to the rest of the village, because she was the one who willed it so. No screams were heard, the killing swift and the destruction absolute.

She heard only the whispers of magic in her mind. They were not as clear as voices, but simply feelings made manifest only to her. Each day from the moment she was born, the whispers were there. As she had grown into sentience, they came in waves, teasing her, begging her, commanding her.

So powerful, they said. *So much potential, let it fester and let it become one great madness to dissolve all.*

The girl knew the madness was not to be trusted, not to be set loose, for when she heard the voices, her body trembled in fear.

The mother and father of the young elf were kind for raising her in Beyhar, far from the Castle of Khirn, far from the peering eyes of the royal family. She was a myth, a tale told to children at bedtime to strike fear in their hearts, lest they get the urge to stray from their beds. Magic did not exist, and if it did, it surely would bring ruin to all. But the girl was born, and therefore magic was born with her. Her parents knew it to be a bad omen, so they kept her safe, and raised her to be kind.

It had all been for naught.

As she stood and watched, feeling the death all around her, the elven girl wept. Sparkling golden tendrils of magic swirled around her in a storm of blood and glory, and she felt utterly sick. Her lips, however, upturned without her leave, and she began to laugh. Her throat choked out a hysteria of laughs, then cries, then laughs once again, her smiles and frowns alternating with each moment that passed. The whispers were so loud she could not hear her own sobs, nor her own laughter. The madness rejoiced, and she felt herself resisting the urge to join. She was the most powerful being in existence, and the world would soon know it.

That is what the girl feared most, now that she had no one to keep her madness at bay.

The door to a ramshackle cottage opened with a creak, the sound of heavy footsteps following. An elven woman closed it behind her, approached a padded chair in front of a dirty fireplace, and seated herself upon it with a sigh. She closed her eyes, breathing in the scent of earth and dust as her head leaned back. Her skin was damp with sweat, her deep brown hair in tangles that tumbled over her shoulders, and she cursed quietly. Although the hunt had garnered no results, at the very least, she had wildberries to show for her outing. It would have to do.

She heaved herself up from the chair and made her way to a crude wooden chest at the foot of her bed. After retrieving a towel and a bar of goat's milk soap wrapped in cloth, she swore again as she felt the meager amount. If there were vendors willing, she would have to trade for more. Shaking off her concern, she reached a hand into the sack full of wildberries, popped a few in her mouth, and made her way back into the woods beyond.

As the woman walked, she entertained the notion of stealing soap, and perhaps a book or two if the opportunity arose. Surely some rich trader would not miss a single bar and some weathered pages. The idea became more appealing with each step she took. Overall, it may save her the trouble of the townsfolk seeing her, and that was certainly a perk. She pictured it in her mind, the image of a bumbling aristocrat fretting over stolen soap, and she smiled.

After some time, she finally reached her destination: a small, clear lake surrounded by deep green trees, with a cave bordering one side of its boundaries. It was one of the few places where she felt a sense of peace, with the calm water reflecting the slowly setting sun. She had the thought that it was perhaps the most beautiful thing she would see in her lifetime. The simple joys were enough for her—not that she had much choice.

She walked to a rock not far from the edge of the lake and placed her towel and soap onto it, freeing her hands. Her fingers began untying the laces of her worn, brown leather boots, and once they were off, she tapped them on another rock, sending lodged dirt tumbling to the ground. As she did so, she thought for a moment that she heard a rustling. Looking around, her eyes scanned the trees, but she saw nothing. She had never seen another soul, human or elven, this deep in the woods, and though her magic could shield the lake, why bother? The voices were trying enough without her using it, so she opted never to do so. Now, with her senses alert and mind wandering, she thought maybe she should have.

The woman waited, listening in silence, but no more abnormal sounds occurred, so she decided to ignore it. After all, there was no force that would be a challenge for her.

With boots set against the rock with her belongings, she moved her hands to the buttons of her shirt. There were only a few at her neck, and as she opened two of the three, the rustling sounded once more. Annoyance bloomed within her, and she could not stand idly by any longer.

"I will ask only once: come out."

From behind a tree, an elven girl emerged, her face flustered. She wasted no time hurrying closer, her voice soft and apologetic.

"I am so very sorry to startle you, my lady. I thought myself alone here until I saw you, and I let my curiosity get the better of me."

The girl approached, her eyes going wide as she stopped in front of the woman.

"My name is Asta," said the girl. "What might your name be, stranger?"

Asta was, in one word, bright, like a ray of sunshine glaring into one's eyes that could not be shielded. But her gaze made the woman freeze in place, shock replacing all other emotions. She was the stuff of legends, of nightmares, and yet Asta was looking at her with wonder. It was not normal.

"Leave."

With slow, soft blinks upon her pale blue eyes, Asta did not waver. "A peculiar name! My lady, in apology, I offer you what I have."

"Go."

She did not stop speaking. Instead, she reached a hand into the large shoulder bag slung around her body and pulled out a small metal tin. "I have only tea at the moment, would that be to your liking? What is mine is yours, as atonement for my rudeness."

The woman was beginning to unfreeze from her shock, irritation rearing its head in its place. "What will it take for you to leave, and never come back?"

Asta startled at her words, as if they had done her a great offense. "Never? Do you own this land you stand upon? Is this lake yours? Is it your right to bar me from this lovely place?"

This girl had no fear, and it was becoming evident she would not be convinced politely.

The woman decided to take a firmer approach. "You will leave, never to return. That, or become dust where you stand, swept into the wind."

Asta blinked, and against all odds, she laughed. "My! Are you sure you are not a traveling performer? You play the role of the villain quite well, very terrifying indeed. My lady... Leave, was it?"

She was teasing her. It was unheard of to tease the woman who housed calamity, and yet Asta dared. If threats did nothing, she would have to play along a bit. "That is not my name."

Asta smiled sweetly. "I could have guessed. Would you be so kind?"

"Valyn," she said simply.

"Lovely!" Asta said, brightening to a level that felt nearly lethal. "A lovely name for a lovely lady."

Valyn froze once again. She could not remember a time someone had called her anything of that nature, anything but vile words and curses. This girl was clearly either new to the world, or ignorant of it.

"Are you satisfied enough to leave?"

"Oh," Asta pouted, holding the tea tin loosely in her hand, gazing at it like it was a puppy lost in the rain. "I assume tea is not to your tastes after all. In that case, could I come another time, with something else?"

"No," Valyn said quickly, putting as much venom in her voice as she could manage. "My threat was not idle. Leave, and forget this place."

Asta's face fell, her blue eyes round and shining, and Valyn bit back the urge to raise her voice. The girl's gaze was far too intense, her words far too frequent, and her energy far too much.

Finally, she sighed very sadly, and stuffed the tin back into her bag, both hands gripping the strap at her chest. "Fine, I will not come here, if it makes you happy. But, I do hope we meet again, sometime soon."

She turned on her heel, and walked away without looking back.

Valyn watched her disappear into the woods, the sun now almost set. Precious daylight had been lost to that odd girl, and it was irksome to a high degree. She shed her clothes quickly, tossing them onto the ground without a care, and dove into the cool water. As she bathed, she watched the fireflies of the forest begin to flit about as darkness fell, though the moon was full and bright in the sky. It was a pretty sight, and for only a small moment, Valyn thought maybe the wasted time had been for the better.

After emerging from the water and wrapping the towel around her body, Valyn washed her clothes, the remains of her soap dwindling. She let her mind go numb, her mundane tasks overtaking her thoughts, reveling in the simplicity. She would not think about Asta, the strange elf who had seemed to have no idea who Valyn was. It was impossible. All knew of the young girl who had demolished an entire village, her small body entwined with golden magic. They said her eyes had been golden as well, that she had looked like a creature sent by death itself, wrapped in the power of the sun. She did not know the truth of it all, only that death was not her master. Death was her life's inevitability.

Chapter 2

Deep purple fingers tipped the last handful of berries into Valyn's mouth, their colorful juice sticky and displeasing. She wiped it off on her pants, leaving a stain she did not care to notice. Her stomach still twisted in hunger, which added to her already foul mood, and the late morning heat beat down on her shoulders as she stepped into the woods. A sheath of arrows rattled quietly on her back, her bow gripped in one hand, sweat rinsing off the residue of the last of her food. She was loath to admit it, but her reason for staying inside for three days was fear.

Though her feet made minimal sound, her thoughts felt loud as thunder.

She had no food left, spent days reading the same few books she possessed, and watched sunrises and sunsets, anxiously waiting for what she could not anticipate. She was afraid of the elven girl. Asta, with hair of deep navy blue, like an ocean from one of Valyn's childhood stories, eyes pale like a cloudy sky, and a personality so bright it burns. She would bring nothing but pain upon her life, and she had let the mere thought of the girl trap her inside the cottage for days. Asta did not strike her as the type to keep quiet, and so their meeting had been the worst possible occurrence. The townspeople would come, and Valyn knew their blood would spill. The whispers said so, and so it would be.

As Valyn kept to the shaded areas of the forest, she let the feeling of the breeze on her face and the plush grass beneath her steps drive out her unease. Food was first and foremost, and she needed to focus. Her mind cleared, and as contentment just began setting in, she caught a trail. Deer tracks were pressed into soft dirt, fresh and hopeful. A good dinner would be in order. She followed the trail, keeping light and quiet, and passing up birds she saw on the way for fear that the deer would wander too far. Valyn wanted the deer, and so she would have it.

A twig snapped, and Valyn dipped behind thick bushes just as the deer felt her presence. She could see it through the leaves, its head poised in her direction, and its movement halted. They both held their breath. Slowly, she drew an arrow from her quiver and hoped that the sounds of the forest would hide any she might make. She knocked the arrow, preparing to stand and take her shot.

In the single moment it took before she stood, Valyn's muscles froze her in place. She watched a flash of ocean waves and the night sky blowing in the air like silk, and she was so entranced she did not register what the color was attached to. The deer trained its eyes on the newcomer, and its apprehension from before vanished. A pretty pale hand reached out and stroked its nose, cooing and whispering as sweet as birdsong. Valyn could not breathe, and it was becoming a problem as her chest began to burn.

Valyn's foot shifted, but it was enough. She had nudged a rock with her boot, rustling leaves on the ground, and the deer immediately turned to run. Asta's eyes snapped over to where Valyn had been hiding, but she would not let her prey go. She stood up in a flash, pulling back her arrow and shooting. The arrow hit its target, and the deer fell to the ground.

They faced each other for what felt like years—Valyn in fear, Asta in what seemed like confusion.

Finally, Asta turned her head to the fallen animal, and for a moment, Valyn felt a different kind of fear. She could not place it, not until Asta's face turned back, her mouth turned in a sad smile.

"A shame," she murmured, but shook her head as if she hadn't meant to say it aloud.

Valyn felt anger boil in her blood. Who was she to criticize her for hunting? She needed to eat, and a deer would last her a long time. Why was Asta's sadness filling her with guilt? She did not care what this elven girl thought, and was about to tell her so until Asta spoke up.

"Pay my feelings no mind, my lady. My troupe says I am sensitive, and I admit they are right. You must live, and sometimes, deer must die."

That was the way of things, and Valyn realized then that Asta was a fool.

All at once, Asta's sad expression shifted to one of joy, and it gave Valyn whiplash as the woman walked over to her, digging around in her bag until her hands surfaced, outstretched to her. "For you," she said. "I was hoping to see you again, and so I have kept it safe until our reunion."

A rectangle wrapped in cloth sat in her hands, and Valyn became perplexed. Without thinking, she grabbed the item and unwrapped it, finding a perfectly new bar of soap.

As if reading her mind, Asta said, "I noticed at the lake you were running low. Please take it, my gift to you."

A gift. How long had it been since she had gotten one? Not since she was a young child, but even then, she could not place a memory. It was unnerving, but she admitted it was far easier than sneaking into town to steal some, or trying to find a willing trader.

Without a word, Valyn shoved the soap in her pocket, and made her way to the deer lying on the ground. Asta followed after her, watching in awe as Valyn hoisted the deer onto her shoulders, gripping two feet with each hand. It was a doe, far smaller than others she had shot down before, but with her mind in tatters and the hot sun above, any more weight would prove difficult.

"Lady Valyn!" Asta beamed, still following even though Valyn was trying to walk away as fast as she could manage. "You are so strong to be carrying that! May I help? I will take whatever you need of me."

Valyn could feel her head begin to ache. "Go back to your home."

"They are not expecting me for some time," Asta responded, as carefree as a sea breeze.

"Then go anywhere else."

As the last word left her mouth, Valyn's stomach growled loudly, and Asta suppressed a grin. She heard the girl rifle around in her pack again, the sound and smell of fruit being cut making Valyn's mouth water. A slice of green pear suddenly appeared in front of her mouth, Asta's delicate hand offering it to her.

"You have your hands full, allow me to help."

Valyn halted her steps, staring at the fruit in abject horror. What was happening? How had she been so unlucky as to pick up some stray elven girl? Why did she offer so much for nothing in return?

Her anger had been at a simmer, but now it was a full boil, steam practically coming up from her throat as she spoke. "Why do you persist? Must you worm your way into my sight just to offer me soap and fruit? To what end?"

Asta somehow did not seem shocked, nor offended in any way. She held the same sad smile as when Valyn had shot the deer, and it only made her temper rise. "I have no purpose, my lady. Not one you would seem to understand, at least."

"I am no idiot," Valyn hissed.

"No, no, of course not! I just mean that if I told you, your belief may not follow."

Asta was speaking in riddles, and Valyn could bear it no more. She began to walk again, picking up her pace and not even glancing in Asta's direction. The girl was still following, but she said no more until they reached Valyn's cottage. *The cottage!* In her anger, she had led her right to her home, now on full display for the one who would surely bring her ruin. Asta seemed to know the woods well, and she would most certainly memorize this place and be able to find her way back. Perhaps she was an idiot after all.

The body of the deer dropped to the ground as Valyn let it slide off her shoulders, and she felt a sticky substance that had soaked through her shirt. Blood was bright upon her cream-colored clothing, the liquid covering one of her shoulders completely and dripping down her arm. Valyn did not care, but of course Asta did.

"Oh, what a mess!" She exclaimed. "Do you need any help–"

"Enough," Valyn spat as she turned to face Asta, staring her down. Valyn was several inches taller, stronger, and far more dangerous than this girl even knew. As she spoke, she felt very far away somehow, like her voice was miles from where they stood. "I need no help. I need no company. I need no babbling girl to turn my brain to mush."

That sad smile, those blue eyes, and the sweetness of Asta's voice were like a brand, burning and melting Valyn's skin. It hurt so bad to see, to hear. "Perhaps," she replied, her voice meek, nearly faltering. "Perhaps people do not know what they need at times. You needed the soap, and so I gave it. You needed food, so I offered it. You needed company, badly, and so here I am. I can see that you do not want these things from me, but you do not know me well enough to know that I give because it is what *I* need."

A silence grew between them as Valyn said nothing, her cold stare like stone, fists clenched at her sides. She would stand her ground, would not argue, would not give the satisfaction of her words. It did not matter. She would pack up and leave for a new forest in a few days' time. Now that this woman knew her name, knew her home, it was no longer safe. Asta could smile at her all she wanted.

Asta broke the silence, gripping the straps of her bag tightly. "I will go. I do hope our paths cross again, Lady Valyn. It seems fate has been making sure of it, anyhow."

She gave no response. Valyn merely turned on her heel, marched into her home, and shut the door behind her. The woman waited awhile before steeling herself, wondering if Asta had camped out there to wait. When she opened the door, there was no sign of the elf, but lying there on a bed of bright green leaves right outside her door were two things. One was the pear, neatly cut. The other was a small bouquet of wildflowers, varying in colors of white, yellow, and orange. They were tied together by a ribbon, a deep blue that matched the color of Asta's hair. Valyn hadn't really noticed, but realized then that it was from her hair. The ribbons had been holding small braids in place, and now one was at her doorstep.

She glanced around again, wondering if Asta would pop out of the woods and catch her the moment she picked something up. No sound out of the ordinary surfaced, even as her fingers scooped up the fruit. She ate a slice, and it was all she could do not to sigh in pleasure. It was a treat, for they did not grow in the forest. She could not remember the last time she had even seen one, let alone eaten one of the green fruits. In just a few moments, it was gone, and Valyn threw the leaves on the ground.

The flowers were still there, the ribbon gleaming in the sunlight.

Valyn left them there, a decision not yet made in her mind. She spent the rest of her day cleaning the deer and cooking its flesh so it would not spoil in the heat, all the while the sun set, and the flowers remained at her door. After a satisfying dinner of venison, her decision was made, though it felt like someone else had made it for her.

She took the bouquet from the ground, filled a cup with water, and set the flowers in their makeshift vase upon her small wooden dining table. The fireplace cast a warm glow onto them, and they seemed almost as if in a dream. Valyn let herself think that. It was a dream, nothing more. In the morning, she would begin preparing for her leave. She needed to be fast, before Asta had the courage to come find her again.

But, just for the night, Valyn let herself forget. When she slept, she dreamt of pear trees and ocean water, of deer bounding over valleys, of their legs breaking and their bodies lifeless. Blood-soaked wildflowers wilted in her hands, and the last thing she remembered in her fitful sleep was a pair of lips, soft and rosy, forming a pitying smile.

Chapter 3

STORM

Six days of drying meat. Six days of deciding what to keep and what to burn. Six days of silence.

Valyn was unnerved despite herself.

She had drawn out her leave, if only out of curiosity, but it seemed that Asta was truly gone. Still, she could not risk the chance of her showing up with the townsfolk, or even other elves. So, with a pack filled to the brim and a mouth working at dried venison, she stepped out of her cottage for the last time. Sadness welled in her chest, but she pushed it down. The emotion would not serve her.

She walked slowly through the trees in the early morning, the sun just peeking over the horizon, the birds in full concert above her head. It was a beautiful send-off, one she did not deserve. She thought of Asta with every step, and realized with a start that the uncomfortable feeling at the back of her mind had been something dangerous; she was worried. Six days had passed with not a trace of Asta—no more gifts at her door, and no more chance encounters. The girl did not strike Valyn as the type to listen well, so the fact that she had followed directions was bizarre. The worry grew the more she indulged it, like an unpleasant rash she couldn't help but scratch.

She had to ignore it, she knew this, and yet, when she saw what looked like a long drag of a boot upon the ground, she followed it. Even as her feet carried her, she told herself to stop at once, to turn the other way, to leave as planned. But the trail was concerning. The boot marks were sloppy, and bushes along the way had been trampled, their leaves toppled to the ground in unnatural ways. Someone had run through here, and a sickening thought began to form in Valyn's mind. She banished it, swallowing down that obtrusive worry. It could be anyone, any lost soul running from whatever they had been fleeing from, and it would do Valyn no favors to follow. Yet she could not stop.

The sky darkened, clouds drifting in to block the light, and the smell of coming rain promised to wash away the trail. As the first drops fell, Valyn began to pick up her pace. Her eyes focused solely on the footprints in the dirt, and it seemed she may end up lost herself, until she finally looked up.

There was her lake, a dark mirror reflecting the growing storm. The trail led to the cave near the opposite side where she was, and she needed to decide then and there. Though being soaked and miserable while walking to an unknown destination would be the wiser choice, the shelter of the cave became more appealing by the second. Sharing the cave, however, was a different matter entirely. If anything, she knew she wasn't above killing the stranger if it was called for. After all, who could hurt *her*?

As Valyn leaned down to step into the cave, her eyes adjusted to the darkness, though not as quickly as the sound of soft crying reached her ears. She stopped immediately, taking in the sight of a head of navy hair, knees drawn up to her face, arms hugged around her legs. Asta, smiling, bright Asta, curled in on herself with a skirt lined with dirt and debris, her usually silken hair tangled and wild. She hadn't seemed to notice Valyn yet, not with the rain beginning to pour, the water quickly soaking Valyn's still-exposed back. She had to choose, and the fact that she had no idea how to comfort a crying girl was making her lean towards leaving. That would be best for everyone. She began to turn her body to brave the storm outside, until Asta lifted her gaze, and Valyn saw there was just as much of a storm inside.

Asta's face did not show any kind of surprise; instead, it flickered with such a profoundly sad expression that Valyn felt her own chest tighten. Her pale blue eyes were red and puffy, and did not leave Valyn's. They wordlessly stared at each other for what seemed like hours, the rain drowning out any other sounds. It was just them and the storm.

Valyn slowly began to inch a bit closer, her body lowering to sit on the ground, so painstakingly that she felt like prey. Asta just watched. Even as Valyn seated herself and looked away, trying to lessen the tense atmosphere, she could still feel the girl's eyes upon her. She had never felt more exposed, with this girl she barely knew looking at her as if she knew every secret, every regret. Valyn squirmed, willing herself to flee, when Asta finally sighed, soft and shaky.

"Hello, Lady Valyn," Asta said, her voice just barely audible over the downpour outside. "What brings you here?"

What *did* bring her there? She hardly knew herself —it was certainly not any kind of logic. She was tempted not even to speak, but she feared the tense silence returning. "You left a trail," Valyn said neutrally.

Asta let out one small chuckle, though it seemed painful to do so. "Do you make a habit of following every trail you see?"

"No."

"Ah, so just mine then?"

Valyn felt her cheeks begin to turn pink, and she hastily went back to neutrality. "I did not know it was you."

Asta smiled, but it did not reach her eyes. "All the better, I would think. If you had known it was me, perhaps you would have turned the other way."

She should have! Every minute that passed felt like torture, Valyn wishing silently that the rain would let up and allow her to leave as soon as possible. She could not stand the sadness on Asta's face, the way her voice felt brittle as glass, or the way this girl, who had always been so bright, seemed to dim. She wanted to ask what had happened, but it would not matter. This would be the last time they saw each other; she had to make sure of it.

Valyn heard Asta shuffle and watched as she leaned the back of her head against the cave wall, her eyes closing. "Rather kind of you, anyhow, once you saw it was me."

Kindness had nothing to do with it; it was simply bad luck, which Valyn was chock-full of. She shouldn't have been surprised, even as her chest remained tight with a worry that she could not banish.

"Don't you want to know why I'm here? What happened to me?" Asta asked.

"No."

"All right then," she replied. "We can rest in silence until the rain stops. I'm too tired for conversation anyway. I just have one more question, Lady Valyn. Indulge me?"

The promise of silence was enough to convince her. Perhaps she could close her eyes and pretend Asta was not there, and the time would pass more comfortably. "What is it?"

"Will you promise to stay with me? Just until the storm passes. I do not think I can stay awake much longer, and I fear being alone here."

A small request, to watch over her as she slept, in return for peace and quiet. Valyn did not have to think about her answer. "Very well."

Asta turned her head, her blue-sky gaze reaching Valyn. "Thank you," she said, and the smile reached her eyes this time.

So, the rain poured on, and Asta slept. Her chest rose and fell softly, her expression peaceful in the darkness. Valyn found herself watching her until the storm began to wane, sunlight returning to the forest, the birds resuming their songs. Valyn stayed still, so as not to disturb the other elf, her dark eyes memorizing the girl's pale skin and gentle features, replacing the image of her tangled hair with how she had seen it days before. Valyn thought that Asta had to be around her own age, with a loving community and days filled with laughs. But was she wrong? What had made her run to the lake, to cry alone in a cave? More importantly, why did Valyn care?

The sound of an animal disturbing leaves outside roused Asta, her lashes fluttering and her body unfurling like a flower. She stretched, and Valyn noticed the winces Asta tried to hide as her body moved, but said nothing. The other elf ran her hands through her hair, fingers getting caught in knots. As she tugged through them, she turned to look at Valyn.

"You stayed," she stated, as if it had been a test Valyn passed.

Valyn said nothing.

Asta let out a long breath, preparing herself. She rose as tall as she could within the confines of the cave and brushed out her skirt. Her hand gripped the strap of her bag tightly, too tightly, as if it were the only solid thing she could feel.

Valyn stood up as well, realizing she was blocking the exit, and stepped outside. Before she could get very far, a cold hand wrapped around her wrist, the touch like an electric shock running up her arm and freezing her on the spot.

"Wait!" Asta pleaded, her grip tightening. "Is this truly goodbye?"

It had to be—Valyn had memorized Asta's face in preparation. The image of her was all she could have, as the real thing was too much. So she nodded, but she could not move her arm away.

Asta's hand began to shake, yet she still clung to Valyn. "I am sorry. It is my fault you feel that you must leave your home. What must I do to convince you I mean no ill will? What must I do to convince you that you can stay?"

Nothing, Valyn thought. She could not trust her words, even if Asta swore on her own life that she would never return to the woods again. Life was a fleeting thing, after all. The townspeople would find Valyn, and they would try to kill her, and in turn, they would all die. No being was a match for magic, but that did not mean they wouldn't try. Valyn already had one town bloodying her hands; she did not need another, not if she could help it.

But when Valyn turned to face Asta, her breathing stopped. Asta was a painting, a piece of art depicting so many things, and Valyn could not begin to keep up. Sadness, anger, pain—it was overwhelming, like she was standing in a deafening crowd. Valyn felt suffocated, but the picture of Asta's face was all she could see, all she could feel. The worry would not leave, and it was terrifying. She could not afford to worry about anyone, and yet there she was. Valyn could hardly remember the last time someone had been in her life. But now, she realized that since the day she'd met Asta, a hunger had begun to grow. This girl could satiate that hunger and become someone to her—if Valyn allowed it.

The voices of the magic began to tickle her mind, sensing her rapid thoughts. *Yes*, they said, *hungry, so very hungry, starving, feast upon her.* Valyn knew their appetite was of a different type, and she took it as a challenge. Perhaps she could have Asta in her life somehow, without giving in to the magic's desires. It was a risk, a gamble, but if she could do it, if she could muster the power to defy the voices, perhaps she could be rid of them.

That was what she told herself, a reason as solid as stone on her conscience. But an unease within her hinted at something else, something far more tenuous. Was it instead that the loneliness and years of isolation had finally taken their toll? It felt as though she was sinking, and now she was desperate for any lifeline presented to her. It was a terrifying thought, that the feeling could control her so. She could not let herself surface from her punishment, let herself dream of a day when she was not drowning. The stubbornness towards the magic was one thing, something with consequences only for the girl she barely knew, since Valyn had no real ties to her. If she died, she died, and while it would not please Valyn, it would be a lesson learned. If she were giving in to her loneliness instead... She ignored the thought.

"I will stay," Valyn said, her voice coming out much softer than she'd thought it would. "You mustn't let anyone know where I am, and you mustn't tell a soul you've met me at all. The consequences would not be on me, but on you. Swear this, and I will stay."

Asta's face brightened to a level Valyn could scarcely believe possible, and her other hand met Valyn's free wrist, the second touch sending another wave through her. "I swear!" she confirmed happily. "I will tell no one. Just our secret."

The words would have to be enough. If not, Valyn would not be the one to pay the price. It would be the girl made of moonlight that would grow dim, and Valyn steeled herself for that fate. What was one elven girl's life in exchange for a town? What was one more demise upon her own hands? Whatever lay in store between them, Valyn knew in her heart that it would run red.

Chapter 4

Just as the morning sun had begun to bleed under the door of Valyn's cottage, a soft rap roused her from sleep. The last two days of racing thoughts had almost settled, but she supposed it was too good to be true. Maybe Asta had given up and left, satiated by the fact that Valyn had promised not to leave. As another knock rang out, she realized that was clearly not the case. She thought for a moment, deciding to stay in bed and let Asta do as she pleased until defeat would urge her to go home. That was the best course of action.

At least, until the smell of bread wafted from the door and all semblance of dignity fled. How long had it been since she had eaten bread? Valyn could scarcely remember her mother's deft hands, red from heat, lowering a steaming loaf onto a table with scattered dishes yet to be cleaned. The memory left as quickly as it had come, leaving a painful ache in her chest. She did not deserve bread, though her mouth watered. She pulled her blanket over her head, stifling most of the fragrance, her stomach protesting with a growl. Valyn ignored her body, attempting to go back to sleep.

There was another gentle knock, this time accompanied by a voice. "Lady Valyn," Asta said, her muffled words just loud enough for Valyn to make out. "The bread will get colder the more you dally."

Leave it at the door, thought Valyn, though she stayed silent.

"It really would be a pity…" Asta said, her tone now almost chiding. "What use is honey without bread?"

Damn it.

Valyn rose from her bed, tying up her dark, tousled hair with a leather cord. Before opening the door, she suddenly became self-conscious and hoped it would not show. Why should she care how she looked to Asta? Just a couple of days before, she had seen the girl sniveling in a cave; surely the sight of Valyn in the morning was not as bad. With that thought comforting her, she undid the hook lock on the door and opened it. Early morning light washed over her and warmed her skin, and she drank in the sight of Asta.

She was wearing her usual clothing, oversized bag and all. Her deep blue hair was cascading over her shoulders, clean and smooth, a welcome change from what it had looked like in the cave. What stopped her were the white bandages she saw peeking out from her sleeves, the expanse of them covering her wrists. Valyn stared, her mind trying to piece together what they could be hiding. Thankfully, Asta did not seem to notice. Her hands were occupied with the bread wrapped in cloth, so to her, it likely seemed as though Valyn was entranced by the loaf.

"Good morning," Asta said brightly, holding the bread out in offering.

Valyn took it with as little greed as she could, but the thought of a warm, soft bite of it was all she wanted. Her hands still swiped it rather abruptly, and Asta laughed. The sound was natural, but Asta's hands jerked just the slightest bit at Valyn's quick movements. She made a mental note to move a bit slower next time.

Asta put her hands behind her back and leaned to look past Valyn's shoulders, glancing curiously into the cottage. "You know," she began, her voice light and playful, "it would be only fair to taste the fruits of my labor."

Valyn's brows knit in confusion.

Asta paused for a moment, waiting for a response, but none came. She sighed, "I made it. I had hoped to share."

The gift suddenly seemed like too much, too fast; the idea of the girl spending time and effort on something for Valyn was unsettling. Valyn tried to shove the bread back to her, but Asta took a step back, shaking her head.

"It was a hope, nothing more. Here," Asta reached into her pack, procuring a small glass jar filled with amber-colored honey. "This is for you as well."

Valyn took the jar more in wonder than anything else, her eyes locked on the way the sun shone through it. Valyn could not remember honey, and again, it truly did feel like a gift she did not deserve. She was about to say so, but held her tongue when Asta took a few more steps back, now out of arm's reach.

"They are yours to do with as you please. I shall come another time, perhaps not so early. I apologize for waking you."

Valyn didn't say a word as Asta turned on her heel and walked into the forest, disappearing into the greenery like a piece of silver lost among emeralds. She should have thanked her, but she did not want to encourage her any more than she evidently already had. So Valyn turned as well, fleeing into her home and closing the door behind her.

Valyn gingerly placed the gifts on her dining table, looking at them for a long moment before deciding that wasting them would serve no one. She unwrapped the cloth, and a subtle warmth radiated from the golden crust that had her stomach rumbling in seconds. Her hands tore into the bread as though she had claws. She lifted a chunk to her nose, smelling it with her eyes closed in pleasure. It tasted as good as it smelled, and it took all her self-restraint not to devour it all that instant. Instead, she tore another piece and paired it with a strip of dried venison. It was delicious, every bite, and Valyn spent the next few minutes in bliss.

A shuffle at the door snapped her out of it, and she brushed the crumbs off her hands, quietly making her way towards the sound. She yanked the door open, just in time to see Asta nearing the trees again. Valyn looked down at her feet, where a pile of fresh blackberries rested upon a pair of large leaves.

Asta's head spun, her eyes connecting with Valyn's. She just smiled and pointed at the berries.

Valyn found herself at an impasse. She should let Asta leave and take all the gifts for herself without any thanks. Her attitude needed to be stern and cold, but enough to keep Asta coming back. She knew these things, but her own words betrayed her.

"Wait," Valyn called.

Asta's face turned from a smile to shock as she pointed to herself, questioning.

Valyn nodded.

Asta's smile could've stopped time, Valyn thought, as the girl nearly skipped over to her.

Though she hadn't wanted to entertain the idea too much before, Valyn let herself indulge as Asta came closer; she really was beautiful.

Before she knew it, Asta was sitting at Valyn's dining table, hands in her lap and her eyes everywhere else. She drank in the sights of the small space: the fireplace upon the wall, one bed shoved into a corner, a wooden chest for storage, and a beat-up cabinet to hold whatever Valyn needed it to. Really, it was just one room with no windows and enough belongings for one very frugal person.

If it was not to her liking, Asta did not say. Instead, she took one look at the loaf of bread with chunks torn off and *tsked*. "I know you own at least one knife," Asta prodded. "Allow me."

Valyn retrieved a dull knife that would get the job done, and set two chipped plates in front of Asta, watching as she cut two thick slices. She then beckoned to Valyn, motioning towards the blackberries Valyn had haphazardly shoved in her pocket. They were relatively unscathed, wrapped in leaves with only a few that had gotten crushed.

Asta placed them upon the slices of bread, then used the knife to drizzle honey on top. Valyn took a seat across from her, feeling utterly useless. Why was Asta serving her like this, and why was Asta so fixated on her at all? She had just determined to ask outright when Asta spoke first.

"Thank you for inviting me in," Asta said, taking a bite of bread.

Valyn just sank her teeth into her own slice, looking anywhere but at the girl across from her.

"My Lady, I have been wondering… How old are you?" Asta asked as casually as if she were at a dinner party.

Valyn figured she could answer questions as long as they stayed surface-level. "Twenty-five."

Asta nodded, swallowing another bite. "Only a two-year difference between us, then. I am the younger of the two of us, if you're wondering."

She had wondered, but did not say so. Valyn did not want to let Asta know how she held onto every word, thinking more and more that her voice was almost canary-like, light and musical. In the peace of the cottage, with a meal shared between them, Valyn felt her guard loosen, and she did not want it to come back up.

"How long have you lived here?" Asta began. "The woods of Setfas are an odd place for you to settle."

Asta was right, but the answer to why had no real reason besides that it was as far from Beyhar as Valyn could get without leaving the land of Khirn entirely. She should have gone farther still, but could not find it within herself to abandon the land she was born in. Though Beyhar was ash and memory now, she could not fully leave it. Setfas was dangerously close to Khirn Castle, the grand structure housing the royal family. Though they knew of her, they had never sent anyone to track her down. Quite the opposite; they never left their castle, not a single one of them. But the woods outside the town were deep, keeping Valyn hidden for years. Until Asta found her.

"Eighteen years," Valyn answered.

A look crossed Asta's face that Valyn could not read. It was almost pity, but something far more complicated clouded her pale eyes. "An awfully long time to spend alone," she said finally, voice barely above a whisper.

Valyn didn't know how to respond, so she kept eating her bread.

Asta's voice went back to normal, though her gaze would not rest upon Valyn. "Your name, it's lovely. Where does it come from?"

That was a question Valyn found pride in answering, and she spoke wistfully, her own gaze drifting to her dagger that hung from a hook on the wall. "In my culture, the children are often named after our ancestors. I was named after my grandmother. I was told she was beloved, and so my mother bestowed the name upon me in the hope that I would inherit some of it. Though I never met her, I heard only praise."

The odd expression from before resurfaced on Asta's face, but her voice was the same. "Kind of them to name you so."

It was more ironic than anything, Valyn thought. She was named after a woman who had seemingly done no wrong, and Valyn would never be able to say the same for herself. She did not like to think too hard about it, so she tried to change the focus by asking, "What about yours?"

Asta waved a hand dismissively, her smile light. "Oh, something about stars or holiness. I never had the chance to ask more."

"Never had the chance?" Valyn wondered aloud.

"I live with an elven Troupe. We have moved from place to place for as long as I can remember. They adopted me, more or less. They have been kind."

Valyn did not pry about the absence of Asta's parents, for it was a raw enough wound in her own life. She looked at the dagger once more, a faint memory of rough hands slipping from her own frail, child's hands fleeing her mind as fast as it had come.

"We came to Setfas not long ago. We stay on the outskirts, trade with the human locals when needed, and I suspect we will move on once the elders get bored."

Valyn had not considered the idea that Asta would be the one to leave. The thought tasted bitter in her mouth despite the sweet berries and honey that coated her tongue.

Asta noticed Valyn's gaze and changed the subject. "That dagger, I have seen it on you before. Did you make it?"

"No," she said quietly, nostalgia getting the better of her. "My father."

If she wanted to press, Asta did not make it known. She just said, "A useful gift. Does it have a name?"

"Rhaina, after my mother," Valyn said as the memory of screams and fire flooded her mind, and she tore her eyes away from the weapon. She tried to calm herself, banish the thoughts, but the magic would not let her. They giggled madly in her ears, a sound only she could hear.

"Are you alright?" Asta's voice felt far away, but it was enough to ground her. Asta was not within her burned memories. She was clean of tragedy, a lifeline pulling her from the darkness.

Though the voices of the magic faded, they still remained in the back of her mind, quietly laughing. "Can we speak of something else?" Valyn asked, hoping Asta would drown out the voices quickly.

"Of course," she replied softly. "May I ask you something?"

Valyn nodded.

"Is it true what they say? That… that you have magic?"

The voices rose like thunder to Valyn's ears, booming hisses and gargling chuckles. *Nothing but a bird*, they said. *She is made of feathers and thin bones, and oh, how we wish to snap them. She would be so lovely in red, a blood moon.* Valyn tried to ignore them, but they had not been so loud in so long, so clear and so tempting. She was afraid, she realized.

In the blur of her madness, a shaking hand rested on Valyn's shoulder, stopping the stinging of fingernails that had begun to bite into her palms, drawing blood. The touch killed the magic rising in Valyn's chest, leaving her gasping for breath. Asta was standing beside her, face pale as she looked at Valyn.

They stared at each other for a long time, and Valyn's shaking slowly settled, though Asta's hands did not still.

After a while, Asta's soft voice broke the silence. "I should go."

Valyn did not want her to. She wanted to feel Asta's hand on her shoulder longer, get lost in her face for hours, feel her hair in her fingers. Valyn had not known just how lonely she had been, and the desperation was more than she could stand. She thought about begging, but Asta's hand lifted and her feet carried her to the door.

The girl's face was blank as she turned to Valyn, stopping in the doorway. "I will be back in two days. Take care of yourself in the meantime, Lady Valyn."

"Please," Valyn rasped, "I cannot be alone."

Asta shook her head sadly. "I know."

And yet, she left.

Chapter 5

The two days passed, the sun and moon making their journeys despite the shattering feelings within Valyn's mind. She felt ashamed, angry, and pathetic all at once. It was as though her own thoughts were not to be trusted, as she had the time to think about everything that had transpired thus far with Asta. Did she crave her attention in purity, or was it simply an act of rebellion? Her thoughts of others' lives were becoming more perplexing as well. One moment she would think to do everything in her power to preserve lives, as she had taken enough in her time, and the next, she would flippantly tell herself killing was a valid course of action if needed. Perhaps the voices were not the only madness within her.

As Valyn wallowed in her bed, buried in blankets up to her chin, a knock sounded at the door. She had no idea what to say after their last meeting, no way to truly explain how warring her thoughts were, but her feet carried her across the floor regardless. Despite it all, she was still lonely.

When she opened the door, Valyn was greeted by wildflowers shoved into her face, the sweet smell calming somehow. She reached up to take them, fingers just brushing Asta's as she let them go.

"Lady Valyn," Asta began, her face so serious it made Valyn freeze up, "I want to apologize for how I left before. The flowers do not begin to express my regret, and I hope you will forgive me."

Forgive her? Valyn was well past placing any blame on Asta, for who out of the two of them had magic enough to destroy everything their eyes touched? Asta had only seen the beginning of Valyn's loss of control, and it had been enough to send her running. No, Asta had merely been a doe in the woods, frightened by the sight of a hunter in the distance.

Valyn opened her mouth to speak, but found her throat dry. How could she ever hope to keep Asta close if she told her just how volatile this magic was? She did not have the pretty words to weave into a tapestry of comfort, not like the girl standing before her. So instead, she held the door open and stepped aside, beckoning Asta to enter.

Relief flooded Asta's face as she took the invitation, quickly making her way to the wilting flowers upon the dining table and plucking them out. Valyn just stood and watched after she had closed the door behind them, the new flowers clutched tightly in her hands. Asta motioned for Valyn to bring the flowers, but she did not move, could not move. In the closeness of the cottage and the roiling within her, Valyn thought if she dared even to breathe too hard, Asta may just flee again. Was it always this terrifying, to have the fear of someone leaving you while they still drew breath?

Asta shook her head with a smile, gliding over to Valyn with such confidence and gentleness it was like she was a feather being carried by the air. She gingerly unwrapped Valyn's tight grip on the flowers and took them into her own pale hands. Before placing them into the makeshift vase, she used one hand to gently squeeze one of Valyn's, and the touch sent a spark through Valyn's body.

"I am not so fragile as to break from one scare," Asta said. "A crack can be mended easily enough, so long as you don't mind the scar."

If only Asta knew how fragile *everything* was around Valyn. Even a city, an entire kingdom, could break past the point of mending. She did not want it to be so, not with this girl. Was that her answer? Was it that lives were expendable, save for Asta's? It felt wrong, and it felt right, and it was all Valyn could do not to scream from her own confusion.

Asta did not release her hand. She instead guided Valyn to the table, sitting her in one of the chairs. When she eventually let go, Valyn's hand felt cold. She wanted to reach back out, but Asta busied herself with settling the new flowers in their place and fetching two cups of water for the two of them. When Asta sat down, her face was serious once more. Valyn took a long drink of water, preparing herself. She had not spoken a word yet, not with the storm of thoughts within her, but she could not drive

Asta away now; it was the only thing she felt certain that she wanted.

"I'm sorry," Valyn blurted out, surprising the both of them.

Asta recovered quickly, though her face still held some trepidation. "What has passed is already a memory, Lady Valyn. I was the one who came into your days only to leave so suddenly, and for that I am ashamed."

"You were frightened," Valyn said.

Asta stopped.

"I…" Valyn hoped her next words were enough to settle her own unease, or at the very least assuage whatever tension Asta still felt. "I will tell you that you were right to feel that way. You should not be in my company, and yet you persist. I wish I could thank you for it, but I know not my own desires and the strength of my control. Keeping company is not… it is not without risk. Your fear is warranted, should it ever surface around me."

The girl listened in silence until Valyn was finished, and the quiet between them grew thick. It felt as though there was a decision hanging like a strand of hair, the connection so tenuous it would snap with no warning. Valyn could do nothing but hope, and that was by far the most dangerous thing she could do.

When Asta spoke, it was with resolve so fierce it felt out of place coming from such a soft girl. Her hair that day was without braids or adornments of any kind, just silken night-sky hair hanging down her back. She pushed some behind her ear, and Valyn watched her slender fingers with bated breath.

"What is a reward without a little risk?"

"So," Asta said, tossing crumbs of bread into the lake, the fish within it swallowing the food eagerly and crowding each other as they did so. "You truly do not know what happens within the villages?"

Valyn shook her head, picking at the grass beneath her fingers. "I see no one unless I need something. Even then, I seek only traveling merchants, or the ones settled as far as they dare go."

The girl sighed, brushing the last of the breadcrumbs off her fingers into the water, scooting her body closer to where Valyn sat on the ground, which made her heart quicken. "The royal family is harsh, to put it simply. Crimes are punished regardless of whether one committed the act or not, and the consequences vary depending on the mood of the guards. If one starving child steals grain for their family, perhaps a guard with a child of his own will simply beat him until he bleeds, sending him on his way. If another finds the boy after a night of drinking, a body will hang in the square within the hour."

Valyn had not ever needed to know the lives of those within the villages, as drawing any attention to herself would end only in pain. The royal family had never bothered her, so she thought to return the favor. It was neither shocking nor expected to hear of the danger in the villages; Valyn did not have a true opinion, for what could she do to stop it?

Asta leaned back, propping herself up with her arms behind her, head tilted up to stare at the bright blue sky above. "I say you may have the right idea, Lady Valyn. These woods are deep and lovely, and so very… free."

Valyn thought so too, but did not say.

"I suppose I have no right to say so. I did not pick my lot in this life, and I consider myself rather lucky compared to the humans. Most of us elves stay in our Troupes until death, our resting place wherever the last of our days ends. The Elders give orders to leave, and we follow. They tell us to stay, so we stay."

The thought of Asta leaving was one Valyn avoided as much as she could. Seven days had passed since they had cleared the air between them, every one filled with each other's company. Some days Asta would stay for only a few hours, and some she would knock at sunrise and leave just before sunset. Wilted flowers would always be replaced, and Valyn had begun to smell their sweetness when Asta was not there. Talk of magic and fear was not broached, so instead Asta told tales of her travels, and Valyn told her stories of her life in the forest. It felt like spring, a gradual warmth in her life beginning to feel more and more blissful. She knew for certain that she did not want Asta to leave, and so she did not think about it.

Out of the corner of her eye, Valyn saw Asta's head turn towards her, and she smiled sweetly. "Enough talk of that," she said, her tone chipper. "I have a task for you."

Valyn raised her eyebrows, eyes resting just a moment too long on Asta's lips, though the other elf did not seem to notice.

Asta sat up and crawled over, turning so her back was to Valyn, shining navy hair touching the ground. "The wind today is making a mess of this," she whined, shaking her head so that her hair flowed in the breeze. "Would you be so kind as to braid it for me?"

Valyn was infinitely glad her face could not be seen, for it must have been quite a sight. In truth, she was practically giddy at the thought, but a drop of fear spread inside her like blood in water. Being around Asta was already enjoyable, enough to keep her happy when she lost herself in it, so she gave up any lingering delusions of more. Yet here Asta was, inviting her touch, and Valyn was not sure she had the strength to say no.

Asta shuffled in place, pushing all of her hair back insistently. "You should know by now that I do not bite, my Lady."

"Just Valyn," she responded. "You needn't be so formal."

Asta paused for a moment, sitting very still. When she responded, her words were slow and careful, as though someone may steal them before they had the chance to be uttered. "Very well... Valyn."

She was satisfied with that, and it gave her enough courage to reach her hands to the dark wave of hair in front of her. When she touched it, she could not help but smile to herself. Valyn slowly began to braid it, more slowly than was normal, but Asta did not seem to mind. She heard soft hums from her, the sound sweet and soft, and Valyn's smile deepened. The sun upon the lake was clear and bright, the sounds of the wildlife around them steady and calm, and Valyn let herself get lost in it all. The moment was so perfect, and she held onto every second that passed, committing it to her memory in hopes it may replace an older one.

It did not last as long as Valyn wanted, for Asta's voice stopped humming, and instead she spoke in a whisper. "How old were you when you lost them?"

Valyn answered quickly, trying to subdue any rising voices that would come. "I was seven."

Valyn continued braiding, and Asta did not speak for a long while. It was long enough that Valyn completed the braid and realized she had nothing to tie it off with. As she was about to ask Asta if she had anything, she spoke once more.

"You were but a child... so young to have been caught in such a tragedy."

"A child with a torch is no different than one with someone grown, once the fire starts," Valyn said, repeating a phrase her father had said to her long ago. It had been something he told her when her magic swelled, and she had cried out that she could not control it. Perhaps he had thought it was comforting at the time, that even someone grown would have trouble controlling her magic, but now it was only a reminder of what she had done.

Asta turned just enough so that one of her eyes connected with Valyn's, and it looked as though it was filled with tears, but Asta blinked them away before Valyn could confirm. "A child does not know that fire burns until it is too late."

Valyn could feel the whispers like an itch at the back of her throat, rising to her head, and so she merely said, "Perhaps," and waited for Asta to turn her face away.

When she did, she suddenly realized Valyn had stopped her task. "Oh! I have nothing to tie my hair with, I'm sorry, I did not realize—"

Valyn then used one hand to hold Asta's hair in place and the other to reach for her dagger. She unwound a piece of leather cord from the handle, snapped it off with her teeth, and used it to swiftly tie the braid. Once she was done, she gingerly placed it over Asta's shoulder.

Asta turned to face her, hands grasping her own hair, eyes fixated on the leather cord. "Where did you get this?" she asked.

Valyn pointed at the dagger that was strapped to its place on her thigh.

Asta looked horrified, her gaze going back and forth from the dagger to Valyn. "I cannot take this! That dagger is so precious to you, I wouldn't dream of using a part of it for something as trivial as this!"

The voices sank away completely, thanks to the restoration of the elves' usual interactions setting Valyn at ease. She chuckled in response, shaking her head. "I would not have used it if I did not approve. Keep it, if you think so highly of it."

Asta looked at her with an emotion Valyn was so acutely aware of it almost hurt: guilt. The girl's voice gave nothing away, and she merely responded, "If you insist."

Valyn could not make sense of it all, so she decided to ignore it. Instead, she looked out at the water for a moment before closing her eyes. The feeling of the sun warming her face was almost as pleasant as the lingering softness of Asta's hair against her fingers.

Chapter 6

As the midday sun sat high in the sky, casting shadows through the leaves above her head, Valyn let an arrow loose. The head sank into its target, a plump wild turkey that had been picking at the ground, unaware of the woman across the glade. It would make a fine dinner, one that she hoped a certain elf would enjoy if she were to visit, as had become their routine. Three more days had passed since their outing to the lakeside, and everything had been as it was.

Valyn was beginning to feel a regular joy in her days that she had not known since childhood. It was becoming less and less alarming, and instead she welcomed it with arms that spread ever wider. The night-sky girl had a liveliness that warmed every part of Valyn, and she had the sense to know when warmth was better than the cold.

Valyn scooped the turkey up by the feet after yanking the arrow from its chest and hoisted it over her shoulder. Her feet were light and swift as she made her way back to her home, an eagerness tightening in her chest the closer she got. Perhaps Asta would be there waiting for her, and the idea made her giddy. She felt like a tree, reaching towards the sun—it was a lovely thought, and she let it carry her forward.

And there she was, glowing skin and flowing hair and a timid smile that could stop Valyn's heart. Turkey in hand, Valyn made her way over, placing it on the ground outside the front door. Asta's eyes flicked to the bird for a moment, but she quickly drew her focus to the woman in front of her, a balled hand pressed against her chest.

"I cannot stay long," Asta said.

Valyn frowned in response, but opened the door in invitation anyway.

The other elf smiled. "Very well, just a quick visit."

They both entered and sat at the table in their usual spots, Valyn realizing that even alone, she never sat in the second chair anymore. It was Asta's now.

Asta reached her clenched hand out and unfurled her fingers to show Valyn what she had been hiding. It was the leather cord from Valyn's dagger, wrapped around a piece of clear, glass-like crystal with the flames of the fireplace dancing on its surface. The crystal was small, but so clear and luminous it seemed completely ill-suited to the rough leather that was tied around it. Valyn wondered if that was what she looked like with Asta.

"For you," Asta said, placing it on the table in front of her.

"I cannot take this," Valyn retorted as she pushed the item closer to Asta and away from herself. "It wouldn't suit me."

Asta laughed, bright and kind. "I think it suits you quite well. I picked it precisely because it reminds me of you."

Valyn raised an eyebrow.

"I mean it, truly!" She pushed it back to Valyn, who pushed it right back. "Is it so impossible to believe a lovely stone can belong to a lovely woman?"

Valyn had no response for that as her mind could not form a coherent thought.

Asta sighed, and then her face lit up as though she had seen some great truth. Before Valyn could begin to decipher it, Asta rose from her chair and went to Valyn's side, pointing at the dagger on her thigh.

Valyn's brow only furrowed deeper, but she removed the dagger regardless and placed it upon the table.

Asta took the crystal and used the cord to tie it to the top of the dagger's handle. When she handed it back to Valyn, she spoke in a whispered voice that was laced with a sadness that made Valyn ache. "Keep it with Rhaina. I have a feeling she would have liked it."

She nodded, placing the dagger back on her thigh and running her thumb over the crystal. It was smooth and cool, and she wondered if Asta's skin would feel the same under her fingers.

Asta smiled in approval, wrapping her hands around the strap of her bag as she eyed the door. "I really must go, I am sorry I cannot stay longer today."

"Must you?" Valyn asked, the words so pleading she wished they had never slipped out. She tried to recover, her next words flowing like a raging river. "I have the turkey outside, you could have some, if you wanted."

Asta's face became strained, eyes never leaving the door. "I am sorry, Valyn, truly. I appreciate your generosity, but the smell of burning meat turns my stomach, I'm afraid."

Valyn did not want to push her, but words flew from her tongue regardless. "I will not cook it with you here, I can wait."

She finally turned to face Valyn, her eyes pained. "Valyn, sweet Valyn, you are gracious and I thank you for it, but the Troupe needs me."

Valyn would not beg a third time, and so she rose from her seat and guided Asta to the door, flexing her fingers at her side to keep from touching the small of Asta's back. Was the feeling of wanting someone as maddening for everyone as it was for Valyn?

As the door opened, Asta took a few steps out, then turned around to give Valyn a small wave. Valyn waved back, watching her go until her body disappeared into the forest. Afterwards, as she was plucking the turkey of its bark-colored feathers, she racked her brain to think of the last time anyone had compared her to anything lovely.

The next day, the two elves sat together in Valyn's home as they took turns helping themselves to another loaf of bread baked by Asta. It had become a frequent ritual that Valyn warmed to quickly, for who was she to turn down fresh food?

"I have been wanting to ask," Asta began, spreading soft goat cheese onto a bit of bread and popping it into her mouth. "Your tattoo, what does it mean?"

Valyn almost sighed in relief at the question, for if Asta brought anything up with a preface of any kind, it was most likely a sensitive topic, but this was one Valyn was proud of. She had done it on herself when she was fifteen years old, staring at her reflection in the lake and hoping it would make her look more like her mother. The simple black line ran from below her bottom lip down to her chin, the same as all the women in her family, or at least that was what her mother had told her.

"My people have tattoos for many reasons, and this is one my mother had, and her mother before her. It is meant to be the mark of a woman, one I had hoped my mother would give me. Regardless, I have it now and I treasure it greatly."

Asta nodded along, listening intently until Valyn was finished. Deep in thought, she took another bite of bread, swallowing after a moment and then leaning her chin in her hand, tilting her head to stare at Valyn.

"It really is beautiful, I think. The sentiment and the look of it—I can see why you treasure it."

Valyn nearly choked on her own bread, though it was not the first time Asta's words had caught her off guard, and it would not be the last. "Thank you," was all she said.

Asta brushed her hands off, peeking at the sliver of light from under the front door as she let out an exhausted sigh. "It'll be getting dark soon, which means I shall have to leave you for now."

Valyn could hardly complain; they had spent almost the entire day together, walking in the forest with light conversation while Asta pointed out different birds here and there. All had been calm and pleasant, and sharing bread was a perfect end to Valyn's day.

Asta stood, dragging her feet all the while as she neared the door, pouting. Even as she turned the handle, she did it slowly to draw out the time it took. Valyn almost laughed, as if she hadn't thought of doing those same things anytime Asta had to leave.

Before she stepped out, Asta turned and said, "Tomorrow, let's go to the lake again."

Valyn smiled and nodded. "Very well, Asta."

The girl froze, wide eyes round as the moon. "Goodness," she breathed, "you've never smiled like that before."

She was right, she hadn't. Valyn could not remember the last time she had smiled with no thought to hold it back, with no hesitation at all.

"And the first time you've said my name," Asta teased.

Was that true? Valyn thought back to all the days they shared, and knew she was right again. How utterly foolish could one lonely woman be?

"Say it again," Asta said, her pale gaze warm in the setting sun.

"Asta," Valyn replied, and a shy feeling enveloped her chest.

The two stared at each other for what felt like hours, neither of them moving, as Valyn felt like lightning would strike her the moment she did. Asta was the first to break the hold on them both as she cleared her throat. "Well," she said, turning to leave. "Until tomorrow."

That night, Valyn slept with the newest wildflowers Asta had gathered upon her pillow, their sweetness a substitute that could only tide her over for so long.

Chapter 7

Something was different about the moonbeam girl, and Valyn could not bring herself to ask about the cause. The day was sweltering, beads of sweat soaking the back of Valyn's neck as she walked just behind Asta. The way to the lake was filled with soft chattering from the girl, but the words did not fully reach Valyn. When Asta had knocked at her door that afternoon, there was a smile painted upon her lips, but a weariness clouded her eyes and there were dark circles beneath them. Her clothing should have been lighter to stave off the heat, but she wore her usual layers, not even bothering to roll up her sleeves. Valyn noticed that the strap of her bag had been sewn together recently, as it had a new stitch she had never seen before. The air about her was strange, and Valyn felt an unease in her bones.

Despite this, Asta was adamant about their lake outing, and Valyn would be the last person to deny her now. The fact that she would give Asta anything she wanted if she simply asked was a development that made her feel weak and giddy all at the same time.

As the two neared the water, Valyn realized with a start that Asta had asked her a question. "What?" she asked.

Asta rolled her eyes playfully, putting her hands on her hips. "Someone was clearly riveted by my words."

Normally, Valyn was rather captivated by anything Asta did, but her concern had overrun her thoughts, and she did not know how to bring it up. Should she? Being around others was difficult, a game Valyn hadn't learned the rules for.

"Anyways," Asta said, "I asked if you had a silly dream that may one day come true."

Valyn shrugged. "I have not given it much thought."

The girl chuckled and shook her head. "What am I to do with you, Valyn?"

Valyn shrugged again.

"Well," Asta began, looking off into the forest with wistful eyes, "ever since I was young, I dreamt of going to a ball. The gowns would be lovelier than any flower and more grand than any gold. The music would feel like happiness of the highest order, and the dancing would be as graceful as any shooting star."

Valyn could never imagine herself at an event like that, but Asta would no doubt rival any dress and any gold.

She looked back to Valyn, waving her hand dismissively. "A silly dream indeed, wouldn't you say?"

Valyn did not agree, for anything Asta wanted could never be so inconsequential. She knew she could not say what was on her mind, so instead she said, "Perhaps one day."

Asta blinked in surprise, but smiled in a way that tugged at Valyn's chest in sadness. She did not respond to Valyn. Instead, she knelt down with one knee on the ground and untied her boot, then switched legs and undid the other, tossing her shoes aside. Savoring the sunlight, she stretched her arms high in the air. While she did all this, Valyn could not look away.

"Come along!" Asta called as she walked to the edge of the lake, dipping her toes with a sigh. "Truly a perfect day for it, what with the sun attempting to set me ablaze."

As Asta began to walk into the water, she did so with all her clothing on, not even reaching to hike up her skirt. "Your clothes…" Valyn said weakly, not sure why she was so worried about them to begin with.

Asta laughed as she responded, "Wet clothes are the least of life's problems."

And what *were* Asta's problems? If only Valyn knew.

She watched as Valyn stepped thigh-deep into the water, her arms reaching down into the depths, and she noticed Asta wince just slightly.

She decided then to follow, if only to keep a closer eye on her. So, she removed her own boots, tossed them with Asta's, rolled her pants up to her knees, and made her way over. The water was pleasantly cool, staving off a bit of the heat, and Valyn took a cupped hand to splash some water on her neck. She kept watching Asta as she fished around, a look of concentration knitting her brows.

"What are you doing?" Valyn inquired.

Asta grinned up at her, pulling out a palm-sized stone the color of a stormy sky. "Looking for stones! You can find true treasures hidden in places others don't dare tread."

If that was what Asta wanted, Valyn would not object, though she found it odd nonetheless. What use were stones other than to be thrown from slings? Even as she thought it, Valyn's hand went to the dagger at her thigh, and she thumbed the crystal tied to it. Perhaps it wasn't as strange as she believed.

Valyn began to shove her hands into the mud as well, her fingers searching for any stones she could feel. Each one she pulled out was dull, colors varying from gray to brown to black. It seemed Asta had no better luck, as every time she found one, she grunted in dismay and threw it back into the water. They stayed like that for some time, traversing the lake only as deep as would cover their legs, exchanging some words here and there while the sounds of the forest accompanied them like music. Even as the sun began to sink farther towards the horizon, they had nothing to show for their efforts.

After a long bit of silence, Asta sighed deeply, tipping her head upwards and closing her eyes. She opened her mouth to speak, but shut it instead, staying in her position while the daylight illuminated her dark hair and white skin like a star come to earth.

Valyn felt a welling in her chest that nearly caused her to reach out, to go to her, to hold her. Though it was her deepest desire at that moment, she did not want to ruin Asta's peacefulness, so instead she did something reckless. Asta was so beautiful and sad that day. Valyn wished only to lift her spirits, and impulsiveness overruled her logic. So, with her back turned, she dove her hands down by her feet, dug out a coin-sized stone, and closed her fist around it.

She willed the magic in her fist to do as she bid, and she hoped it would happen fast. The radiant golden tendrils encircled her closed hand, alighting the water as though a lamp had been lit in its darkness. As the magic pulsed within her, so too did the voices.

A stone for a bird, they said, *as an arrow to a deer, as an eclipse to the moon, make it so, make it so!*

Faster, the magic needed to be faster, and so Valyn pushed it harder. The gold grew until it snaked up her arms, the sparkling of it deceptively lovely.

More, they hissed, the sounds similar to the cackling of a crow, deafening in her mind. *Hungry, starving, consume her, be fed, be full.*

"Valyn?"

And the voices stopped, sliding away like smoke from a window, quieting slowly as the golden tendrils dulled to nothing.

Valyn opened her hand, and there sat a navy stone, a sparkling blue covering every inch like a thousand diamonds. It was the single most beautiful item Valyn had ever seen, and yet she still felt it was not worthy enough.

When she turned to Asta and lifted her gaze, she was not sure what she saw.

Asta was there, and she was as still as the tree trunks surrounding them, but instead of roots grounding her, Valyn saw it was fear. Her eyes were wide, lips slightly

79

open, and hands white-knuckled upon the strap of her bag. Valyn could not make sense of it, could not understand what had paralyzed the girl. She held out her hand, the stone shimmering in the fading light of the sky.

"For you," Valyn said.

Asta did not move. Her eyes darted to the stone, then back to Valyn.

Valyn took a step forward, and Asta took one back in kind.

They looked at each other again, Asta with the same wide-eyed horror, and Valyn could not begin to imagine what her own face looked like. Inside, she felt pain. It was a pain she had only felt once before, years ago, in the crumbling remains of a place she had once called home. Devastation, she realized. As she did, the telltale sign of her magic began to swell in her chest; it was a sour feeling, as if acid were coursing through her blood. But she did not want the golden light to give her away, to make her lose control as she had when she was a child. The voices rose, and she tried to ignore them and their pleas. She was no longer a child, and she would not let the magic rule her.

Before the magic rose too high to quell, Valyn watched as Asta reached a shaking arm out. Her delicate fingers gently took the stone from Valyn's hand and clenched it in her fist. She drew her arm back, slowly, carefully, as though Valyn may explode at any moment. Asta placed it in her bag, her eyes never leaving Valyn.

"Thank you," she said, voice hoarse and weak.

The magic and madness quieted once more, and Valyn took several deep breaths, drawing in as much air as she could. She wanted to collapse onto the ground, but the two were still standing in the lake, and she was unsure if moving first would frighten Asta, so she stayed.

After a long while, Asta's leg slid cautiously to her side, towards dry land, and Valyn gave her a simple nod. As the girl moved away, she still did so at a measured pace, keeping her gaze on Valyn even as she retreated. Valyn just watched right back, a horrible feeling trickling through her.

Once Asta reached the grassy lake edge, she retrieved her boots, slipped them on, and stood still for a time. It was as though she were trying to make a decision, and she could not come to a conclusion. Valyn felt sick.

"Asta," Valyn called, finding that her voice was scratchy and very near tears.

The girl winced as though she had been hit.

"Asta," Valyn called again, a bit louder, a bit more desperate.

Again, she recoiled, but her feet began to move in the opposite direction.

"Please," Valyn begged, but the word was too soft for Asta to have heard.

Then, Asta turned around and began to walk away.

Valyn knew she had made a mistake that she could hardly have known the consequences of. She felt like she knew nothing, that her logic had fled simply because she had been overrun by one moment of wanting to please the girl she loved, and yet the action instead had driven her away. It was maddening in a way that made her chest ache with self-loathing. Would the magic never cease to take from her?

Perhaps that was her fate, to live with power enough for a god while she still had nothing at all.

Chapter 8

Nightmares plagued the lonely woman, the days of solitude stretching into nearly a week. She had waited, then searched their frequented spots in the woods, and finally sat at the lake's edge, staring at her own reflection until the moon came out. The sight of it was too much now, a reminder of a girl so similar in likeness. The last wildflowers on her table had long since wilted, but she left them regardless, not daring to toss them out. She slept with the dagger under her pillow, one hand gripping the handle and stroking the crystal until her eyes could no longer stay open. Night after night. Day after day.

Valyn could stand it no longer on the seventh cycle. What had she to lose now? She opened the chest at the foot of her bed, dug out a wrinkled black cloak, fastened it at her neck, and pulled up the hood. The night was warm, with a slight breeze shaking the leaves and muffling the sound of any movement she may make. She left just as the moon overwhelmed the sky, slipping out of her cottage and making her way towards Setfas.

Asta did not want to see Valyn; that much was clear. The woman knew the feeling of wanting to avoid people all too well, but she craved closure more than her lungs craved air. She needed to see her, one more time at the very least. Asta had been hiding something at the lake, and even if she never told Valyn what it was, perhaps a last look at the girl would abate Valyn's nightmares.

Her dreams were filled with old and new memories alike, though the new would twist into unrecognizable things that would wake her with a start. The day at the lake was a frequent visitor, and that dream either did not change, or the voices won and all Valyn would see in Asta's place was red. Over and over the memories would repeat, and Valyn felt as though her mind would snap like the twigs beneath her feet as she neared the town.

She had never gone this close to Setfas, never been near enough to clearly see the humans living there. It was strange to see a place like that, still whole instead of smoldering. Valyn wanted only the company of the elf girl who she knew was part of the nearby Troupe, but to find her, she needed to find the humans.

Valyn began searching the outskirts of the town. The sounds around her were unnerving, so unlike those of her forest: merriment from a tavern echoing into the night, a beggar shuffling in their sleep on the street, a cat jumping from rooftops in search of prey. Despite her unease, she would do anything to find Asta, and so she continued.

Finally, she spotted a tall elven man, dressed in loose brown clothing and carrying a drawstring bag to the town. Valyn watched as he disappeared into the streets, and she traced his footsteps back to where he had come from. It took longer than expected; they had set up their camp farther from the humans than Valyn thought. The place was filled with makeshift tents, all of them still and silent in the night air. The only sound came from the crackling of a fire in the middle of their setup, the flames slowly dying. She had hoped it would be easier to tell where Asta might be, but it seemed the elves valued their sleep and did not stir for as long as Valyn sat and waited. She had waited so long, in fact, that the elf from before was approaching with his bag considerably lighter, though Valyn could hear the *clink* of coins within. She didn't want to speak to anyone, didn't want to let any soul know she was so close to the town, but she had no other choice.

Quickly, Valyn slunk over to the man, approaching him from behind until she was near enough to reach out and touch him. She lunged forward, restrained the man's arms behind his back, and pulled him behind the cover of the trees. Before he could cry out, she gripped his wrists in one hand and slapped the other over his mouth. His muffled yelling warmed her hand in a way that made her recoil in disgust, but she held fast.

"Asta," she whispered harshly, "do you know of her?"

The man became confused, his voice quieting a bit, though his struggling persisted.

"Nod if so," Valyn ordered.

In his one subtle nod, Valyn felt her whole world brighten. "Where is she?"

He tried to speak, but the hand upon his mouth covered his words too well.

Valyn sighed. "I will allow you to speak, but if you call for help there will no longer be a life to save."

The man nodded in understanding. Quick as a flash, Valyn removed her hand, unsheathed her dagger, and pressed it to his neck. He was silent for a moment, his body now trembling instead of struggling.

"Where is she?" Valyn repeated in a hiss.

The man gulped, his words stuttering and panicked. "T-the cells I-I'd assume…"

The cells? Why would Asta be there, in custody of the human guards? Nothing made sense and it only made her temper rise. "And where are these cells?"

He described the path to the squat building that housed the guards, stating that the cells were underground, dug into the earth long ago. Valyn listened intently, but one thing was grating on her. Why was Asta being held? Why hadn't they killed her?

"What did she do?" Valyn asked, allowing a bit of softness in her words.

"I-I don't know," he replied, and she knew he wasn't lying.

It was as good an answer as she was going to get, so she pressed her blade against the man's skin, and hovered her mouth next to his ear. "Tell no living soul of this meeting. In her name, I will not shed her people's blood tonight."

He nodded vigorously, and Valyn let him go. He tumbled to the ground, clutching at his bag and scrambling to his feet as quickly as he could manage before running back to his Troupe. Even if he did speak of Valyn, he did not have her name, nor her face, so she decided to push her anxieties away for the night. Asta was her priority. Nothing else mattered.

So she followed the directions of the elven man, weaving between buildings and avoiding any humans who were out and about. It was a simple enough task, as the night had been growing later and later, the moon high above as if to mock Valyn. Daylight felt so far out of reach, just like Asta. The moon would not be mocking her for much longer.

The guard building was unassuming indeed, a wooden structure just as plain as the rest around it, though the door had an iron lock on it that was deceivingly intricate. It mattered not, for there was no structure and no lock on Earth that could keep Valyn out. She let her magic flow from all the pores in her body, fingertips tingling and stomach roiling. The golden tendrils wrapped around her arms, legs, torso—every inch of her body. The voices rejoiced, but she would not be swayed. Not that night.

She then closed her eyes, and began to sink into the ground.

The feeling was like floating as she became nothing, her eyes open and seeing only dirt in front of her. Her legs moved in a walking motion, but her form had no solidity, so she glided forward instead. After only a moment, she phased through a stone wall, and stepped onto a dirt floor. She looked around and saw iron bars lining the space on either side of her. Some cells were empty, and some held curled-up bodies in the darkness. Valyn kept her magic around her, shielding her from the eyes of everyone but the one she wanted to see her.

It did not take long to find her, even in darkness. Asta was sitting in a corner inside a cell, back resting on the wall, head dipped down into her knees, arms shielding her head. Her clothes were dirty, her hair a tangled mess, her feet bare and crusted in dried blood. It was a sight that sent tremors of rage through Valyn, and the voices feasted upon it, like maggots to flesh.

And though Valyn was silent, Asta looked up.

Her face was streaked with tears as she squinted to focus on Valyn's glowing form. Once she came into view, Asta's eyes widened, her mouth agape.

Before she could speak, Valyn stepped through the iron bars and into the cell with Asta. She had wanted closure, but to leave Asta there was to sentence her to death, and she would not allow it. Asta could hate her, despise her, but she would do so alive.

"Come," Valyn said, outstretching a hand wrapped in gold.

Asta's whole body shook at the movement, her limbs shrinking back in fear.

"Please," Valyn begged, "I will not have this be the last place we see one another."

The girl shut her eyes tight, taking in deep and rasping breaths. "Do what you must, but I cannot look upon you."

It stung deep within Valyn, but she agreed. "Alright then."

With a loving gentleness only for her, Valyn wrapped an arm around Asta's shoulders, then another under her knees, picking her up and holding her to her chest. Asta clung to her, still shaking with eyes shut tight. The magic trembled at the contact, and the voices erupted in a chorus of jeers and pleas, Valyn's senses flaring in a madness she desperately needed to quell. Despite Valyn's very being begging for Asta's blood, begging to feed upon her life to quell her own hunger, she held tight to the girl in her arms. She walked back to the stone wall, her feet taking them into the ground beyond, and they rose to the surface.

The night had almost passed and the sun was rising steadily into the sky. Valyn tried to subdue the magic, but the voices persisted, and her own arms began to shake.

No, no, no, she begged them. *Not her, anyone but her.*

Asta released her tight grip on Valyn, urging her to let go. She did, gladly, watching as Asta blindly stepped onto the ground, wincing in pain from the wounds on her feet. Valyn wanted so badly to pick her up again, to spare her the pain, but she did not trust her own desires. Instead, she unlaced her own boots and set them on the ground next to Asta, not daring to touch her again.

"I'm sorry," Valyn said softly. "Live well."

She could feel her control slipping through her fingers like a snake, too agile to fully grasp. The voices would not stop, and she had no intention of being around Asta when they acted upon their wants.

As she turned to leave, she felt cold skin brush her forearm. Asta's fingertips were frigid and quivering, as though the simple brush was all she had the strength for.

Valyn turned and saw that Asta's eyes were still closed, though tears managed to squeeze out, dampening her cheeks. She drew her hands into her chest, holding them there together. "Thank you," she murmured.

Those two words were the last she had heard at the lake, and though the sound of them again still hurt, she savored them. She savored the sound of her voice, the color of her hair, the softness of her skin, all the things she had come to know and want. The memory would have to be enough.

"Anything for you," Valyn responded.

"Then..." Asta said, "will you wait for me?"

Valyn would wait a thousand lives and a million births of a new world for her, but she simply whispered, "Yes."

Chapter 9

A young elven girl of seven years old rubbed mud-covered hands along already dirtied pants, marvelling at her work. She had dug a line of water from the flowing river within the town of Beyhar over to a large colony of ants. Her eyes followed the flow of it, slowly but surely inching ever closer to the insects, crawling in and out of their home none the wiser. The girl's feet slowly crept along at the same pace until the water finally reached the anthill. She watched as the water overflowed, soaking the mound of earth and all the bugs within. Their bodies floated along, getting swept away by the current, unable to cling to any solid ground. The child watched, and she began to feel an unease within her chest that she did not have the knowledge to name.

The whispers within her mind took up all her inner thoughts anyways, melting the unease into something more familiar.

Look how they drown, the voices said, cooing in tones akin to metal scraping against metal. *Insignificant, the world turns still, unneeded are they.*

The girl supposed that was true. She still lived even as they died, even as the water soaked through her shoes, the same water that suffocated them. Still, something her mother had told her nagged at her mind.

"We take life only when we need to," she explained. "The birds that fly and the deer that bound draw breath just the same as we do. We take from them what we need, and honor their sacrifice."

"What about people, Mama?" the girl had asked.

Her mother had paled, eyes widening. She cleared her expression before her daughter could sense anything amiss, coughing to clear her throat. "That is not quite the same, love. We would never hurt someone unless our life was truly in danger. Do you understand?"

The girl thought she did, but the voices began whispering so sweetly, so surely, that she doubted her mother's words. *Kind*, they said, *until she knows. She will know, and where will you be?* The thought etched a great fear into the child's heart.

Before the girl could respond, her father had walked into the house, hefting a lamb over his shoulder. With a large smile, he used one calloused hand to pat the child's head, beaming down at her. When he withdrew, he leaned over to kiss his wife, presenting the animal.

Her mother rose from her seat as she rolled up her sleeves."Outside with you," she said playfully to her daughter, tickling her sides and eliciting a giggle from the child. "Dinner must be prepared. I will come get you when it is time."

The girl nodded vigorously, though when she stole a glance at the lamb, a strange feeling welled in her chest. Her young mind did not dwell on it as her father handed her a large wooden spoon, his tanned and weathered face never losing its grin.

"Go dig something up from the riverside." He winked, knowing that she would inevitably get filthy, which caused her mother to groan in protest.

The girl smiled back, gripping the spoon in both hands and rushing over to the door as her father held it open for her.

"Valyn?" her mother called.

She stopped, turning to glance at her as the setting sun cast a warm glow inside the house.

"*Asavakkit,*" her mother said. "Do you remember what it means?"

Valyn wracked her brain, her small voice letting out a long *hmmm* in thought. Finally, she shook her head, tangled hair swaying at her shoulders.

Her mother laughed and replied, "It means '*I love you.*' Go have fun, my sweet."

Now, watching the last of the ants wash away, the child had nothing so lovely on her mind, only the feeling from the voices that she had a word for.

Hunger.

Once she thought of the word, it was as if the flow of the entire river had burst into her chest, unrelenting and overwhelming. She began to hyperventilate, the air only choking her more, and her small hands clutched at her chest. She could not scream—she could only fall to her knees in the pool of water, lifeless insect bodies crushed under their weight. Even as she heard her father's voice from the door of her home, she could not utter a sound besides rasping breaths. She felt his strong arms lift her to his chest, rushing her to her panicking mother. Their concerns did nothing but cause the hunger to grow.

More, the whispers urged. She could not remember when they had gotten so strong. She thought of the ants and wondered why she had killed them in the first place.

Without realizing it, her breathing became even, deep, and steady. Her eyes stared unblinking at the ceiling from where she lay in her bed, the face of her mother out of focus even though she was so close. She was crying, too, and Valyn could not hear her. All she heard were the voices urging *more more more*, so loud her ears began to ring.

"Ants," she whispered, unable to hear even her own voice. "I'm sorry."

The repeating word was all she heard. It had to stop. She had to make it stop.

What do you want? She thought desperately.

It is what you *want,* they replied. *You're hungry, so hungry, you starve, and the bugs will never be enough.*

What would be enough? She asked.

And the echoes of *more* began again, louder, faster.

She felt tears running down the sides of her face, and the touch of her mother's loving hands wiping them away only made them flow all the more.

Valyn turned her head to glance at her mother's face, and the hand that had been so gentle pulled away in an instant. Confusion clouded the child's face, for what she saw in her mother was so foreign to her. She did not know what it was, did not have the right word.

The voices obliged. *Terror,* they said. *See? We do not lie, we knew it, we knew it, we knew it.*

The sounds around the child became clearer, as if the whispers had quieted themselves to make sure she heard.

"What is it?" her father asked, grasping at her mother's shoulders. Though when his eyes rested upon Valyn, that same expression painted his features.

"Her... eyes..." whispered her mother in response.

The child felt a great heat spreading over her body, and a shimmering gold enveloped her.

"No," her mother murmured, "no, we have to calm her. How do we calm her?"

Valyn's father knit his brows, and seemed to make a decision. He reached a hand down to touch her shoulder, and the moment he did, his skin began to burn. He yanked his hand away, and the terror set in his eyes once more.

The husband and wife took a step away from their child, and that was when the thread snapped.

Valyn remembered only fleeting moments, like the way her body moved seemingly without her controlling it. The house had gone up in flames so quickly, just like the rest that followed. The smell of burnt flesh seemed to soak into her clothes. The only thing keeping her from retching was the constant flow of words from her lips, a repeated phrase that could not be heard by any of the dying.

"I'm sorry," she cried, over and over. "I'm sorry, I'm sorry, I'm sorry."

All the while, even as sick as the sights and smells made her, the hunger that had been growing in her body was fading, and the magic rejoiced.

They burn, the voices cheered, *they burn, and yet you live. We feast now, we will feast always, you will feast forever.*

The child did not want to. Hadn't her mother told her this was wrong? But her hunger pained her so, and it was bliss to satiate it. She had never felt stronger.

That is, until the golden magic around her carried her, floating, back to her burning home. Her mother was silent upon the ground, blackened just the same as the walls of their home. Valyn's father was still breathing, weakly, half his body smoldering and melted.

That is when Valyn did retch hard enough to expel what little she had in her stomach, but once she was done, the magic dragged her to him regardless. She tried to close her eyes and found that she couldn't. The magic wanted her to look upon him, chest wracked with coughs and his once-sure hands shaking.

With his one intact eye, her father focused on her, and she could not tell what sort of look was on his face, for only half remained. Even in the state he was in, his unburned hand feebly reached to his thigh, where his dagger rested.

Valyn knelt beside him, her voice hoarse as she uttered, "I'm sorry."

Her father pressed the dagger into her hands, wrapping her frail fingers around the handle. He could not speak, but up close, Valyn could see his single eye well with tears before it became unfocused, staring up at her.

The child took the dagger and stood to watch the rest of the village going up in pillars of smoke in the sky. She cried heavy tears that flowed in a constant stream until the morning sun rose with the new day. She cried and cried, trying to remember even as her cries broke into laughter, only for tears to overtake her again and again. Her father had told her about fire, and her mother had told her about life; those words she remembered clearly. But there was another, a word from their language that her mother had reminded her of just before she left the house to play. What had it been, and what had it meant? It felt important, and in the charred remains of what little was left of Beyhar, it was the only thought that kept her from true insanity.

Valyn awoke to a knock at her door, the sound startling her out of bed. She blinked rapidly, her body soaked in sweat from the nightmare she'd had. Nightmares about her hometown had never been so vivid, not until now, and she wondered why. As she pondered, another knock sounded, and she jumped again. She cursed, running her hands through her hair to push it back while making her way to the door. There was only one person it could be, and she was equally consumed by both dread and happiness.

There stood Asta, bathed in noonday sun, just how Valyn liked her. Though she liked Asta in any light, she thought. She wanted to smile, but the look on the girl's face was ashen, with the most serious expression she had ever seen her wear. Nervousness gripped Valyn's heart like a vice, but she did not show it.

Asta looked up at her with those lovely moonstone eyes, and Valyn was stuck in place. "Come," she said. "I have something I must confess."

Chapter 10

The lake glistened in the quiet of the forest, the life around
the two elves seeming to hold its breath just as Valyn did.
They sat together upon the ground, an arm's length of room
between them, Asta with her knees drawn into her chest
and Valyn with hers crossed. Neither looked at the other,
and the tension between them continued as the minutes
passed, strong as any stone. Valyn had a sinking feeling in
her stomach rooting her in place, and she dared to even
blink. What if she closed her eyes one moment, and the
next Asta was gone?

They had walked to the lake in silence despite Asta
telling her they needed to talk. Despite the way the girl
acted around her now, and despite everything, Valyn let
herself cling to some happiness, at least. Asta was there,

and that was enough. No matter the outcome, seeing her there, safe and lovely, was enough.

After a half hour of silence, Asta began to stir. Valyn heard the shuffle of her clothing, and out of the corner of her eye, she watched as Asta stretched her legs in front of her, hands in her lap. The girl did not look her way, gaze fixed only on her own hands. She took a deep, shaking breath before reaching into her bag. Her hands shook all the while as she retrieved what she needed, her arm moving towards Valyn. Valyn did not look at Asta's face; she merely watched as the item in her hand dropped to the ground between them.

There, upon the emerald grass, was a piece of wood. At least, that was what Valyn assumed it had been. It was the color of coal, and looked as though it would crumble to dust with too much pressure. Valyn could not make sense of it.

"That is from the handle of my father's axe," Asta said, her voice soft as a breeze. "He was a woodworker, and my mother a cook. I have fond—though fuzzy—

memories of the smell of wood and potatoes alike. It was…
simple."

Valyn did not respond, and did not dare to interrupt
her. She found that she liked hearing about Asta's past. She
liked how it seemed as if, for one reason or another, Asta
wanted her to know. She held onto that thought.

"I was five years old at the time," she continued,
tone changing ever so slightly from wistful to something
more melancholic. "They had been trying to find a Troupe
for us to join, for the kingdom had become far less tolerant
of elves within town walls. My mother would have to give
up her shop, but safety was more important. I heard her say
that to my father on more than one occasion: 'Safety, we
must stay safe.'"

Valyn's chest ached for whatever fate she knew Asta
would tell her of. Still, she did not ask, and merely let her
talk at her own pace.

"I was with my mother. We were gathering fruits
from the trees outside the town. She would hold me high
over her head, my hands grasping at the highest fruits I
could manage. I remember that so clearly, the way the

apples felt in my hands, the way she laughed as I dropped a fair amount on my own head. I am thankful, at least, that I carry those memories with me still."

Valyn knew what that was like, to have some small memories seem as clear as the daytime sun. She took a chance, and reached a tentative hand over to Asta, trying to rest it on her arm. Asta let her, but Valyn could feel her stiffen, still not turning to look at her.

"That day, it took time to reach my father. But we were not close enough, not nearly. My mother set me on a large tree branch and told me to stay until she came back. I did, and I watched her run back to town. Instead of my mother coming back to hold me, to carry me back home, the smell of smoke arrived first."

Valyn felt her blood freeze within her.

"You would know the smell well, I'd imagine. I have never been able to stomach cooking meat after all this time. Still, even as I heard screams, I stayed. Even as the sun rose with the new dawn, I stayed. My mother had told me she would come back, and I had no reason to doubt her.

Perhaps my father needed help, and they would both come back for me when he was well enough."

Asta paused to take a breath and shuffle her body away from Valyn's touch. The empty feeling permeated all of Valyn's insides.

"I've no idea how long I sat in the tree. A passing troupe found me there, took me down, and we walked the charred streets while I told them my mother and father were waiting for me. In an act of kindness, one man agreed to take me to my home. I led him there by hand, telling him of the joy my mother would feel once I told her I found a Troupe for us. He never said a word to me, not as I found my home in embers, not as my hands dug through the ashes and found my father. He did not speak even as another elf lifted me into her arms and carried me away, the man retrieving the piece of wood from my father's axe, crumbling in his burnt hand."

Asta took the memento into her hands, carefully placing it back in her bag.

"And eighteen years passed, Valyn. Beyhar burned eighteen years ago, and here we sit."

Valyn could not breathe. She stared at Asta, eyes wide, body trembling. *No*, she cried in her mind, *no, no, no*.

"You were supposed to be a monster," Asta said, finally turning her head enough to glance at Valyn. "Everyone said so. A being so terrible and powerful that none could look upon you and live. All my life since then, I shivered in my bed night after night thinking about you. It mattered not. I had to find you."

Valyn could not speak a single word. She felt as though the weight of the Earth was crushing her into dust.

"We came here to Setfas, and I met you. And instead of a beast, I found a lonely, solitary woman. All the better, I thought. A monster is not so easily slain, but a young woman could be."

Asta took a long breath.

"That bread was meant to poison you, back when I brought it for you. But I never got the supplies, and so I waited. I had to steal them, and I wasn't caught, so all the better. But every meal I made and every day I spent with you was not at all how I imagined. I wanted you dead, Valyn. I wanted to take your life by my hand in return for

110

all those lost, all those *I* lost. And come to find, you were a child, same as I had been, one who had lost her own family in that very fire. A child with unlimited magic, a power which had never been seen—how were you meant to control it?

But here we are. You saved me from the prison I put myself in, with no concern as to why I was there in the first place. The touch of your hand makes my heart leap, and I am so confused and afraid. Your magic is eating you from the inside and I fear I have no way to stop it from doing so, so why have I stayed by your side? Why, when I fear you as much as I love you?"

Valyn felt no more worthy than dirt upon a king's shoe, a stain upon a glorious gown, a pebble among an ocean. She spoke finally, words sure and quiet.

"Do it, then," she said. "Take my life, and be freed."

Anger flashed on Asta's face; it was a true, seething anger that Valyn never imagined could come from such a gentle girl. "Do you not understand? No longer are you some myth to keep me terrified in my bed. You are an object of desire like I have never felt. You could so easily flick your wrist and paint my blood upon the ground with that horrid gold, the color of everything tainting you, and I am afraid. But even despite my fear, I want you. I cannot make sense of my own mind, but I know this: if I were to kill you now, I would follow soon after."

Desire. The word echoed in Valyn's mind like a song, and the butterflies in her stomach grew so strong it was all she could do to keep herself still. She did not care for her own life. She cared only for Asta, her soft, pale skin, and her dewy blue eyes that focused on her with such intensity she felt she may turn to stars on the spot, lost in the sky of Asta's gaze. The voices were silent, as if they had never been there at all.

So she leaned forward, and Asta's face turned from anger to bewilderment. Valyn froze.

But Asta's expression cleared, and she took one of her delicate hands, cautiously placing it on the back of Valyn's neck. She pulled her closer, their lips a breath away, a question hanging between them.

Valyn knew the answer. She did not have to think. Her own hands went to Asta, gripping the sides of her hips and pulling their bodies together. Asta let her, and closed her eyes.

When their lips touched, Valyn immediately wanted more. She deepened the kiss, and Asta let out a soft sound that had her mind reeling. She held Asta's body tight against hers, Asta's hand entangling in Valyn's hair, the other wrapping around Valyn's waist. Time seemed to stop for them, nothing reaching them but the sound of their breaths on one another's lips and the feeling of their warmth. Valyn hoped all her words would pass through their contact; the fact that she was sorry—and had been ever since Beyhar—and the truth that she would do anything for Asta with no question. She kissed her desperately, with all the longing and years of solitude melting away like snow in spring. Asta was rooted steadily, anchoring them both as the temperature rose between them. It was an entirely different loss of control than anything Valyn had ever felt. Instead of the nauseating fear of magic forcibly taking command, desire was something she was more than willing to surrender to. She would happily let it take over her mind and body.

Asta pulled away first, breathing heavily as she rested her forehead upon Valyn's. They sat there for some time, bodies still flush, eyes closed, simply feeling the presence of each other. Valyn had never felt happier in all her life. She decided to run with it, to let her happiness carry her like a river.

"Come home with me," she whispered to Asta. "Stay."

Asta chuckled breathily, wrapping her arms around Valyn. "I may, if you promise me something."

"Anything." And she meant it.

"If the magic ever overwhelms you, give me the chance to calm it."

Immediately Valyn's eyes flew open, panic rising in her chest. No one could calm the insanity of the voices. They merely ebbed and flowed, and when the tide came in, everything on shore would drown. She was about to say so, to tell Asta that if that were to happen, she needed to run without turning back, but Asta shook her head.

"Let me try," she pleaded. "It scares me so, but you are worth it. We all must face our fears eventually."

Valyn could not bring herself to agree with words, so she nodded with great hesitation.

If Valyn ever had to face her fears, she knew life would no longer hold meaning, for if she truly lost Asta, the world would know no peace.

Chapter 11

INVITATION

Days went by in a blissful haze, like a dream Valyn never
wanted to wake from. Every brush of hands and every
stolen glance felt like the first, sending sparks beneath her
skin. Asta had many questions regarding Valyn's thoughts,
and she answered without hesitation. Most were the girl
seeking reassurance that Valyn was truly past the reason for
their initial meeting. Valyn could not care less; her
happiness at present was more important. She felt she could
get past anything for Asta, that nothing else would matter
so long as Asta continued to love her. But Valyn had a
question of her own, a thought that had been nagging at her
mind. Even as Asta's head rested upon Valyn's lap, stroking
the ends of Valyn's hair as they looked out over the
lakeside, Valyn's brows knit in question.

Asta seemed to sense Valyn's thoughts as she turned her head to face her. "What is it?" she asked, her face breathtakingly lovely in the orange and yellow hues of the sunset.

Valyn sighed, resting her hand upon Asta's cheek and rubbing a thumb along her skin. "I have been wondering for some time... why were you in that prison? How did you get in?"

The other elf bit her lip in thought before speaking in a more serious tone. "The dealing and buying of poison is against the law. I had simply told them I bought some, and they were happy enough to believe an elf confessing to a crime."

"But why?" pressed Valyn. She could not understand why Asta had subjected herself willingly to such pain and confinement.

Asta smiled sadly, reached up a hand to meet with Valyn's, and rested her fingers there with a light gentleness. "Why do you live in seclusion? Why deny companionship?"

Valyn then understood, completely and utterly. Fear of hurting others, fear of losing what you hold dear—they were exactly her own thoughts. Even so, Asta's willingness to lock herself in a cage just to keep from hurting Valyn was alarming; her own pain was of no consequence. Instead of saying so, Valyn leaned down and brushed her lips against Asta's.

"Never again," she said softly. "You will not be caged for my sake."

Asta lifted herself upright, stood and brushed out her skirt, and outstretched a hand to Valyn. "I cannot say it was a pleasant experience, so I will do my best."

Valyn smiled up at her, taking her hand as they began to walk back to her cottage, the sky darkening behind them. As the night sounds of the forest rang out, Valyn focused only on the feeling of their linked hands and the presence of Asta's body next to hers. She glanced over at Asta more than a few times, and when she was caught, Asta would smile, threatening to stop what little breathing Valyn could already manage.

Once they arrived at the door, Valyn tried to pull her hand away to allow Asta to leave, but the girl gripped harder instead. The woman was puzzled, though not disappointed.

She wanted to ask what was wrong, but Asta spoke first, stepping so close that Valyn could smell the subtle scent of mint upon her skin. "Are you so eager to be rid of me tonight?"

Valyn was anything but, and the question confused her. "No, of course not."

"Then invite me in."

She felt the air between them change, as though a piece of flint had been struck and fire began to bloom. Even without a real fire, Valyn felt her skin grow hot. "You need no invitation," she replied, swallowing down the welling feelings in her chest.

Asta smiled coyly, an expression Valyn could get used to. "Very well. Shall we?"

Valyn did not need to be asked again.

The moment she opened the door and slammed it shut behind them, she took Asta's face in both hands and kissed her fiercely. Asta took it in stride, opening her lips and making a pleased sound that sent a shiver down Valyn's spine. Before she could do anything else, Asta pressed herself against Valyn, her back now to the wall as they clung to each other like wind-whipped leaves in a storm. She was getting swept away, and she had never felt anything as joyous. Even as she tried to fully lose herself, fear still pricked at the back of her neck. She wanted to be gentle, to take it slow, but her desire was so strong she worried it would be too much.

Valyn slowed her pace, though it ached to do so, and Asta pulled away instantly, leaving Valyn gasping for breath.

"I have said it to you before and I shall say it again: do not treat me as if I will break. I am not in the mood to deny you, nor myself," Asta said, her voice stern.

Valyn still hesitated, resting her hands on Asta's hips and gripping them with barely any strength. "Are you sure?"

In response, Asta's hand reached to untuck Valyn's shirt, her fingers running up Valyn's back. With just enough pressure to feel it well, her nails scraped against Valyn's skin, eliciting a soft moan from the woman.

All fears dissipated, and Valyn quickly locked their lips together in a torrent. She saw Asta as soft and beautiful, a flower whispering in the breeze. But this version of Asta was entirely different: begging, hungry, almost violent. Even so, it enthralled her, and she craved it wholly. Her hand reached to tangle in Asta's long navy hair, and when she pulled at it, Asta's head faced upward towards the ceiling. Valyn's lips moved to her cheek, her jaw, her chin, then finally down to her neck, all while Asta sighed in contentment.

It did not take long for Valyn to eventually pull Asta to her bed, where she looked down at the sea of dark hair and pale eyes. She was lost, fully immersed in the girl before her, and she took a moment to etch the vision into her mind. A blush upon her pale face, eyes half-lidded, marks on her exposed collarbone, and all of it for Valyn.

"You're perfect," she said.

Asta wrapped her arms around Valyn's neck, pulling her down into an agonizingly slow kiss. "So says my love, so it must be in her eyes."

Valyn shook her head, dusting kisses over any bare skin she saw. "No," she breathed, "say my name instead."

"Valyn," Asta replied, her hands pulling up the woman's shirt. "My Valyn."

So Valyn forgot every pain life had bestowed upon her; she forgot about the magic, and about the world itself. Nothing mattered more than Asta; nothing was so lovely or so exquisite. For at least that night, with skin against skin and her breath one with Asta's, she let herself be happy.

The two elves slept wrapped around each other's bodies, the rising sun heralding a new day with the light peeking from the crack under the front door. Valyn awoke first, and she roused Asta gently, brushing loose hair behind her ear. She gazed down at her with a smile plastered to her face, the expression impossible to be rid of. Especially as the girl's eyes fluttered open, a yawn escaping her lips, Valyn's smile only grew.

"Good morning," Asta mumbled, nuzzling close into Valyn's chest.

So Valyn let her stay like that as long as she wanted. The day would march on regardless.

As the time passed, Valyn ran her gaze over Asta's skin and realized that with so much of it bare before her, she was able to see things she hadn't before. Healing bruises colored her arms, as well as old, scarred gashes that peeked from her back to the tops of her shoulders. Valyn thought back to the lake and their rock hunt, how Asta had never shown her body despite the water and the blistering sun. Even farther back, she remembered the cave in the rain, and how the girl had been so meek and afraid. The thought of anyone hurting Asta, leaving ugly marks upon her skin, caused Valyn's chest to clench in anger.

Had it been the villagers, abusing an elf as they so often did? After rescuing Asta from the underground prison, it seemed likely, but the thought felt bitter in her mind, as if it was only halfway to the truth. She wanted to ask when Asta had been hurt, by whom, and why, but seeing the girl's peaceful face in slumber calmed her rage, if only slightly. She would find out soon enough, and she would have them dealt with—but not now.

Another hour or so passed before Asta finally began to move, much to Valyn's disappointment, as gazing at her serene sleeping face had been very pleasant. Asta leaned over to kiss Valyn's forehead before standing up and gathering her things. As she did so, her eyes darted to and from Valyn multiple times, clearly trying to find the right words.

"What is it?" Valyn asked, hoping her prompt would help.

"I have something I must tell you, but you must let me finish before you reach a conclusion," Asta replied.

Despite her anxiety rising against her attempts to push it down, Valyn nodded.

"The Troupe has told me they are moving on," she began. "Tensions within the town are high, and with an escaped criminal in their midst, they think it best to leave."

Valyn waited, but a sinking feeling stirred within her.

"They have been good to me ever since… ever since that day. But I am a child no longer, and I told them I would make a decision of my own."

Valyn held her breath.

"When you asked me to stay, did you mean it in the way I hoped?"

Valyn nearly cried out of joy and her emotions shook like an earthquake in her chest, but all she could muster was a teary-eyed nod.

"Then… if you'll have me, I would like to stay."

As if it was even a question.

Valyn stood up and wrapped Asta in a tight embrace, her face sitting in the crook of Asta's neck. Never again would she be so alone, as long as Asta wanted the same.

The girl laughed, hugging Valyn just as tight. When they released each other, Asta gathered the last of her things and led Valyn to the door by hand. "This will be my last day with them," she said. "I will gather all my belongings, and then I will return. Will you manage the day without me?"

The last had been said as a joke, but Valyn felt doubt nonetheless. No day would be right without Asta, but she had goodbyes to make and Valyn would not keep her from them. "I will wait here for your return."

"I should be back by sunset." Asta stood on her toes and kissed Valyn's forehead, then moved down to her lips. Valyn missed the touch immediately as Asta turned away, taking a few steps out into the green of the woods, a star among the leaves.

"Asta?" Valyn called.

The girl turned.

"Asavakkit."

"What does that mean?" asked Asta.

Valyn smiled broadly, folding her arms and leaning against the doorframe. "I will tell you when you return."

And she watched as Asta grinned and shook her head, waving to Valyn as she made her way back to the Troupe.

The promise of a future, one with someone beside her, was making Valyn think that all the years alone had been worth it all along. Once Asta was settled, Valyn would see to it that the ones who had caused her pain before would become nothing but dust in the wind. That was right and just. She knew it to be true as a whisper, soft as a drifting leaf, echoed in her mind and urged her towards violence. Even if the magic felt wrong in her hands, ensuring Asta's safety was all she cared about. Her own discomfort did not matter; she knew she was right. She had to be.

Chapter 12

Valyn watched the last slivers of sunlight fade from her doorway, the sky that had been warm now turning cold. She sat with her elbows propped on her knees, chin resting on her hands, and cheeks flushed with anticipation. The moon was turning brighter by the second, just a crescent of silver upon a sky that seemed so much more vast to her now. She thought of all the things she could do for Asta, the life that awaited the both of them from that day onward. She wished time would pass faster.

But the minutes seemed to stretch, the stars beginning to blink into view, and Valyn felt a prickle of anxiety. *Sunset*, Asta had said. She had promised to be back by then, and yet the night sounds of the forest slowly began, a concert of crickets and owls echoing around Valyn, but not quite reaching her ears. She could not listen past the beating of her heart growing louder and louder. The woman rationalized, telling herself that Asta was just running late, and that at any moment she would see starlight hair to match the sky nearing her. She smiled at the thought.

But the hour grew late, and Valyn began to panic.

She rose to her feet and snatched her cloak, dagger, and boots, assembling them as quickly as her shaking hands could manage. The feeling of dread swelled in her chest, despite her efforts to calm it. The voices were not helping as they egged her on, whispering to her, though there were no words to make out, only eerie hisses. She pushed them down as best as she could, but it had never been her strong suit, so they merely continued as she shut the door behind herself.

The walk to the village was quiet for a time, the woods dark and shadowed by scarce moonlight and thick greenery. The familiarity of her home faded the closer she got, and the nearer she walked, the faster her uneasiness festered. She was thinking up any number of reasons for Asta's lateness, but all thoughts faltered as the sounds of the townspeople reached her. She had only been there at night one time before, but the sounds of a large crowd were clearly out of place. She broke through the trees and saw torches glowing all around, alighting the surrounding buildings and streets. There were no wandering humans, no elves out for trading, not even a dog begging for scraps. Valyn could not see any living soul, but she heard them.

Valyn began to make her way towards the center of the town, her steps light and soft, though she thought anyone may hear her heart beating in her chest as the sound hammered in her own ears. As she flattened herself against a stone building just behind the gathered crowd, she dared to take a moment to breathe. It caught in her throat the moment she heard a booming voice cut through the chatter.

"Here stands the accused! Come, come! Do not be shy, girl."

Valyn peeked from around the corner of her hiding spot, and her blood ran cold.

There was Asta, lovely, shining Asta, barefoot and bleeding. She was upon a raised wooden platform being held up by guards in full metal armor as a human man in a lavish outfit stood at the center. Asta's head was downcast, her starlight hair cascading down her face, its usual smoothness and luster now dull and tangled. Her usual upper layers of clothing were stripped down to a single white shirt, and Valyn could see red just reaching to her sides and shoulders. Her feet were pooling blood beneath her, and her skirt was covered in dust as though she had been dragged upon the ground.

"This elf," began the man in the center, "conspired to murder the Royal family! She had been in custody, but due to the sly nature of her people, she escaped the grasp of punishment. No longer will she evade justice."

Valyn's mind was reeling, her thoughts spinning in circles so fast she could not keep up. Asta did not care enough about the Royal family to orchestrate their deaths. How could she, with them locked in their towers for years?

"No!" A voice cried in the crowd.

An older elven man began to push through the gathered humans, and the man upon the stage sneered down at him.

"You question the truth?"

The elf trembled as he looked up, his voice loud but afraid. "I told you before, she means no ill towards the Royal family! The poison was meant for the devil in the forest, you must find it and kill it before we all meet our end!"

Valyn began to shake.

The human man scoffed, his hand signaling for a guard to whisk the old elf away. "We will deal with the villain in due time, if it even exists. This girl before us must face the law, decreed by the King himself."

The elf struggled against the guard who pulled him back through the crowd, his words sweeping over the quiet whispers surrounding him. "She must be kept alive! She knows the location of the devil, ask Gideon. Gideon!"

Another elf materialized from the sea of people, and Valyn knew his face. It was the same elven man she had questioned about Asta's location the first time she had ventured into town.

"He speaks true," Gideon said, addressing the attendant towering above him. "I have seen the monster that lives in the woods, felt her blade upon my skin, heard her voice hunger for blood. Asta knows, she told me so."

For the first time, Asta showed signs of life as she lifted her head. Her eyes were gleaming with tears, and though it seemed to take a great deal of effort, she spoke.

"He lies," she rasped, "I take my punishment."

Gideon reeled back at her words, his brow creasing in frustration. "I saw her! You told me you were leaving the Troupe, and when I asked why, you said you had some lover in the woods. Who else could it be but the devil?"

The crowd began to murmur to each other, but Asta spoke again, silencing them.

"I lied," she said, her head sinking down again. "There is no one in the woods."

"Aha!" Crowed the man on stage. "She admits it. Begone now, before I call yet another guard to drag you people away."

The old elven man disappeared from Valyn's view, but before Gideon moved, he made one more plea. "Didn't you see we punished her already? Her involvement with the devil was beaten out of her; we made sure. Why else would we discipline one of our own?"

Valyn felt hatred, scalding hot inside her. The Troupe had caused Asta harm because of her, and yet Asta had taken it all just for more time together. She had promised Valyn a future and gone back to say her goodbyes, despite the pain they had inflicted. Valyn couldn't stand it. The poison meant for her, the beatings she should have taken instead—everything rose higher within her and the voices lapped it up gleefully. She did not stop them.

The man on the stage sighed. "Take him away. I have no use for myths, for she will not escape her fate regardless. So decrees the King."

Gideon did not struggle as another guard whisked him away.

Valyn's eyes rested on Asta again, her feet frozen in place as she felt only fear and anger. She no longer heard the words spilling from the attendant's voice, the sound muffled as if she were underwater. Her breaths were heavy and ragged as she watched a wooden stump be placed upon the center of the platform, and a man with a large sword stood beside it. The two guards holding Asta up dragged her to it and forced her to her knees.

And whatever had frozen Valyn snapped.

She stepped out from her hiding spot, and as if Asta sensed it, she lifted her head to gaze out on the crowd. When Valyn dropped the hood of her cloak, Asta's pale eyes found her instantly. At first, Asta smiled, a sadness beyond words etched into her lips. But in a moment, her face turned grave.

Her lips parted, and her words came out in a yell that snapped all the heads gathered there to her. "No! They do not know what they've done! They do not know the consequences! You must not become the devil they scorn you to be! Please!"

But oh, how she wanted nothing more. She felt it from the top of her head to the tips of her toes, an all-encompassing power that felt like being burned alive and like being in Asta's embrace all at the same time. She just barely registered that her feet no longer touched the ground, that everyone was now far below her as they gaped at the golden being above them.

The voices within her head erupted in ecstasy, and they begged her for blood. She no longer had thoughts of her own. There was no more pain, no more loneliness— only hunger. There were no faces down below, no humans or elves, just ants, like all those years ago. The difference now was that she no longer favored fire. Instead, she yearned to feel it all with her own hands, to douse herself in the last of their fleeting lives.

No longer did she have mortal desires. There were only the voices; she was them and they were her, one single entity that knew only one thing: hunger. Nothing else mattered, and there was not a force in existence that was their equal.

In the last coherent thought she could register, Valyn heard only the magic whisper to her sweetly, and she listened with bated breath.

Dance, they said, *dance in blood and gore and feel it rot under your feet.*

And she had no mind left to deny them.

Chapter 13

DANCE

For added immersion, listen to Hole-dwelling by Kikuo while reading this chapter, and imagine it as a dance to the music.

Valyn felt the skin of a stranger under her hands split like rotted bark from a tree, the sound of it sloughing to the ground just a dull thud in her ears. The more tissue and meat she felt in her hands, the more desire swelled within her. She needed more, more touching of flesh, more beneath her feet, more carnage in front of her eyes. The sight of blood erupted in spurts like flower petals and fell to the grass below in a blanket of red. It grew thick and sticky, but she refused to step foot in it. Her feet instead stayed just above the ground, and she began to dance as a fleeting thought brushed past her mind; hadn't she known someone who wanted to dance? It sounded lovely.

She could not make out any faces, nor any sensations save for the limbs she took in her grasp and the overwhelming urge to keep moving. The Khirn Castle loomed tall before her, and Valyn wanted to see the shivering insects inside, but all in due time. She had a performance, after all. The voices sang so sweetly, like an orchestra just for her, and she smiled. She took the hand of someone next to her, rested the other on their waist, and began to lead them.

Every digit she held began to crackle like lightning, quick and abrupt, until they went slack. The body she held there convulsed, and it too slumped, bent impossibly backwards. So she let go. Not the right partner, it would seem.

The next struggled, but it was delightful to Valyn. She laughed as if she had been told a wonderful joke, and she spun them around as they danced. The arms tried to wrench away and finally gave up when they were no longer attached to the body from whence they came. Valyn dropped the arms after the legs plopped to the ground below, torso following along like a waterfall of flesh.

Another dancer in her grasp simply shook, their body trembling uncontrollably. It made for a very poor routine, and Valyn became annoyed. With both hands, she lifted them into the air, but they would not calm. So be it. They split into two halves easily enough, and that was that.

Valyn danced with every person she came across, the joys of their swaying and twirling always souring. Every new partner disappointed her, but still she tried. There was one who was perfect; she knew it deep in her bones, if only she could remember. The voices only sang louder, urging the show. She obliged, the head of her newest partner falling from their neck in a grand fountain that shot up above her head, and she gazed at it in awe.

Valyn's feet took her closer to the castle, dancing all the while. Her arms reached out, her feet delicately stepped over obstacles of flesh, and her hair flowed around her in brown and gold and red. She was drenched head to toe in ruby, bathed in gore like she would bathe in the light of a sunny day, or the coolness of a full moon. How lovely she must be, how her partners must cry out from joy. She heard them occasionally in the back of her mind, as if she were hearing them from far away, and it made her grin ear to ear.

The people she encountered started to become larger and heavier, dressed in silvery armor, and they looked so gorgeous as blood leaked from between the plates and whatever viscera managed to slide out from their shells. She noticed weapons in their hands: swords, spears, crossbows, and all manner of other feeble attempts to stop her recital. They did look fun, though, so she tried some out. A spear spun in her hands effortlessly as she incorporated it into her movements. The tips of each weapon always found purchase in a body, but she grew tired of them quickly, as she preferred using her hands.

The door to the castle opened before her with but a glance, and a cavernous hall spread in front of her. Rich tapestries thick with dust hung on the walls, and a long, hardly-walked-upon rug led up to something that sent a shiver of anticipation through her. The throne of the King of Khirn was there, and upon it was a cowering old man. Two younger men stood at either side, while an old woman and a teenage girl hugged each other tightly behind the throne. The men were standing tall, brave, and armed. Valyn could not see their faces any clearer than any of the villagers she had danced with outside, so she knew they were not any more supreme. She was the only being that was powerful, the only thing to exist that was worth a throne.

So she stepped forward, and the Princes brandished their swords. The King lifted a trembling hand to point at her, giving a silent command. Valyn laughed, and she laughed for some time. With only a thought and a clap of Valyn's hands, the two women behind the throne became nothing more than meat piled on the stone floor. All the men in the room turned to watch the blood run, and she let them. Of course, only for a moment, as she was already bored with them and their joyous screams. The Princes met the same fate as the women, and yet the King did not rise from his seat. It didn't matter, because whatever Valyn wanted, she would have.

Her dance picked back up as she closed her eyes and drifted to the throne, humming as she did so. The King's body did not deserve her hands, so the golden tendrils lifted him instead, wrapping around his neck and squeezing so tightly that when Valyn opened her eyes to look, his own were no longer within their sockets. His body was unsightly to begin with, now even moreso. She flung him away in disgust, blissfully out of sight.

Valyn stood in front of the throne, drinking in the sight of it before finally settling down upon its polished wood. Her body leaned back into it as she propped an elbow on the chair's arm and made a fist to rest her head on. She closed her eyes, calling on her magic to thread its way across the ground like tree roots spreading into the earth. With the reach of the golden tendrils, she sensed whoever drew breath still. The few stragglers were dealt with swiftly, a snapped neck or spine all that was needed.

It was not enough.

Despite the fact that all the villagers were dead, she was still hungry. It ached in her stomach as if she had swallowed a rock, the heaviness becoming more and more uncomfortable. The voices told her she could have more, that she should have more, that this not being enough was exactly right. Would it ease her ache? *Yes*, they said, *yes yes yes yes yes yes yes yes yes yes!*

Valyn stood up, her hands turning to fists at her sides as she called to her magic more, more, more. It was more than she had ever drawn, and yet it did not tire her. In fact, it enthralled her. Just how much power had she been keeping at bay? How much could she really do, if she simply tried? Was she ever meant to hold it back in the first place? It did not matter. Nothing else mattered but her hunger, and she yearned to be fed. So she stopped her focus, and instead let the power wash over her like a gentle rain.

In the middle of the Royal Hall, she imagined a grand ball, so vivid she half wondered if it truly was real. Musicians played beautiful, winding music, and she wore a golden dress that shone like the sun. Rich food and drink made her mouth water, and the faceless attendees around her were jovial. A particularly pretty song began to play, string instruments lilting a melody that brought tears to Valyn's eyes. She reached out for her dance partner.

A pale, slender hand slid into hers, and it was as if happiness had become truly tangible. The swish of a midnight blue gown of sapphire and topaz drifted in front of her, the soft sounds of jewelry like bells tickling Valyn's ears. When she lifted her head, a girl of unparalleled beauty stood before her. Her hair was adorned with silver and diamonds, and a circlet of silvery leaves sat atop her head. It was the only face Valyn could see, and she knew without a doubt it was the only one that mattered.

The girl smiled and did a curtsy as the rest of the guests took their places around the two of them. Everything was drowned out but the music, the girl, and the glittering gold that flowed from Valyn, the magic pouring from her endlessly. Her free hand grasped the girl's waist tightly and held her as close as she could manage while they danced. She spun her, lifted her, and twirled her with their joined hands high above their heads, and Valyn wanted to stay in that moment for eternity. Nothing else could compare.

When the music ended, Valyn realized the throbbing hunger had gone away completely, just as the golden magic made its way back to her, settling within her body.

She smiled and drew the girl to her in an embrace. "Asta," she whispered.

But Asta's arms did not encircle her as they should have.

And the ballroom melted away like mist, the scents and sights and sounds all slowly disappearing. Even the voices dulled to a hum, until their sounds became nothing at all. Valyn began to feel a coldness in her spine as the scene faded.

When reality finally came into view, she did not register it. She took in her surroundings, though it was as if she were seeing it through frosted glass, unreal and unfocused.

There was the bloodied Royal Hall, and there was her throne. It did not feel like a triumph to gaze out at it, not when a weight rested in her arms that didn't fade away like the rest of her fantasy. Valyn knew one thing for certain, for she had done it herself, but she put off acknowledging it. She had something else to address.

She hadn't spared a glance at what she was holding, not until her mind cleared enough to truly see. Her knees gave out, her body sank to the ground, and she began to shake. She shook so violently her eyes had trouble focusing, and the loosening grip of one hand was so weak she wondered how she could still hold anything. But she reached and felt soft, silken hair beneath her blood-soaked fingers. In a desperate attempt to see clearly, she held her breath, and looked down at her lap.

There, resting on her legs, was Asta. She seemed to be asleep, as her eyes were closed and she did not move. Valyn's hand drifted to cup her cheek, and she froze when their skin met. Why was she so cold? Valyn let out a breathy laugh, realizing Asta was wet, so of course she was cold. She conjured a blanket from nothing, without even stopping to think about it. Valyn covered Asta with it up to her chest, and smiled down at her. But the blanket was getting damp. How was that happening? Valyn watched as a stain bloomed on the blanket where Asta's chest was, the fabric soaking up a liquid that puzzled Valyn. She peeled away the blanket, and she stared for a long while. Something so ugly didn't belong on Asta, the dark redness oozing from a hole that gaped up at Valyn from the left side of the girl's chest.

The voices had been silent, but they rose again now in just a whisper, so soft that Valyn struggled to hear it. But she ignored them. Even as they told her that she got what she wanted, everything she wished for. She was no longer hungry, and she had taken the heart of the girl she loved. What more could she desire?

She finally formed the words of her actions in her mind. As she felt nothing but misery there on the cool, rigid floor, holding a body to her own that may as well have been just as lifeless, she cried. Her wails shook the castle walls and echoed outside to the ears of no one at all. Valyn was the only one who knew of her own pain, the only one who was left to mourn anything.

Upon the world she stood, only she remained to draw breath.

Chapter 14

Valyn did not move from the floor, did not dare disturb Asta's body, and did not look away from her face. She may have been there for days, perhaps even weeks, because she could do anything. With magic, she could stave off hunger, and she could keep the body upon her lap just as it was. She spoke to her in hushed tones whenever she had a thought. Valyn told her about the owls she saw in the forest at night, asked if she ever wanted to see the ocean, and confessed that when they had promised to be together, she hoped they would travel. When she waited for a response that would never come, Valyn would stop speaking and sit in silence once more.

Valyn stroked Asta's hair as words tumbled from her lips during one of her more potent moments of delusion. "I do not know what to do," she said. "Won't you tell me?"

Valyn knew she couldn't.

"I have all the power in the world, my love, and in the end, it truly was a curse."

No words of compassion came, but Valyn still spoke.

"What good did my birth bring? Had you still been here with me, that would have been enough to warrant my life. When it is just me, purpose no longer holds any weight."

Being met only with silence still, Valyn's chest began to tighten, and anger infected her words.

"This magic can do anything, anything at all. I merely need to think of something, and it appears before me. My hunger wanted to feast on life, so I took it all. But Asta, my Asta, what use is magic when I cannot have you?"

Valyn closed her eyes and gritted her teeth, wanting so badly for it all to have been a nightmare, and not for the first time. But every time she opened her eyes, the scene was the same. Anger would not serve her now, for she had none to blame but herself. Her greatest fears had all come true, and she had never been strong enough to stop it. Perhaps it was fate, and she had always been destined to this end.

She began to let her mind wander through her memories, settling on the image of when she first met Asta. A chance encounter, she'd thought. Asta had been searching for her all that time to exact revenge, and Valyn would have let her. It would have been better that way, but no matter how desperately she wished, she could not turn back time.

And with that thought, Valyn's heart seemed to stop in her chest.

Her breaths came in ragged and shallow, and her vision blurred with tears.

Now, her heart began to race. She held Asta to her tightly, her own sobs making her back shake. With every part of her mind, every ounce of will she possessed, she uttered a single word.

"Please."

The voices erupted so loud her eardrums popped, but she held fast. They screamed at her, cursed at her, their hisses like blades in Valyn's head. She ignored them, squeezing her eyes shut and rocking back and forth. The golden magic radiated, encasing both her and Asta in a light so bright it would have blinded anyone who could gaze upon it, had there been another living soul left.

Before, the magic had felt effortless, but now the more she willed it, the more painful it became. It was as if the magic did not want to grant her wish, but she would have it regardless. She let the pain rise, the feeling searing every cell in her body. Valyn was screaming, her own cries so deafening it could have been the only sound left in the world, but she kept going. This suffering was deserved, and she had no right to push it away. Her throat grew hoarse, but still she pushed. With her eyes closed, she could see nothing, focus on nothing but her own agony and the feeling of Asta's body still in her arms.

In a blink, it was as if someone had snapped their fingers, and all at once, the hurt disappeared. And so did Asta.

Valyn collapsed, unconscious and numb, with Asta being the last thought her mind had been able to form.

Chapter 15

The door to a ramshackle cottage opened with a creak, the sound of heavy footsteps following. An elven woman closed it behind her, approached a padded chair in front of a dirty fireplace, and seated herself upon it with a sigh. She closed her eyes, breathing in the scent of earth and dust as her head leaned back. Her skin was damp with sweat, her deep brown hair in tangles that tumbled over her shoulders, and she cursed quietly. Although the hunt had garnered no results, at the very least, she had wildberries to show for her outing. It would have to do.

She heaved herself up from the chair and made her way to a crude wooden chest at the foot of her bed. After retrieving a towel and a bar of goat's milk soap wrapped in cloth, she swore again as she felt the meager amount. If there were vendors willing, she would have to trade for more. Shaking off her concern, she reached a hand into the sack full of wildberries, popped a few in her mouth, and made her way back into the woods beyond.

But the woman froze just as she reached the lake that was her destination.

She knew this day.

Valyn looked down at her hands as they trembled. With a shaking breath, she willed her magic to appear.

And nothing happened.

She tried once more, bracing herself for the voices within her mind, but all she heard were the sounds of the woods around her, and then, rustling sounded from behind.

Valyn turned around, peering into the trees. She saw nothing, but knew she was there. As she tried to speak, no words came, her throat closing as she pushed down cries of joy. She had no clue what to do, only that she had been dealt a fate now that she would spend the rest of her life trying to deserve.

Valyn managed to quell her emotions enough to call out, though her voice was laced with disbelief. "Asta?"

The girl stepped out from the trees, her moonlight hair shining in the sun. Her face was puzzled as she stepped forward. It looked as though her mind was at war, struggling to make sense of everything around her. She took several more steps forward, narrowed eyes focusing on Valyn's face. When she stopped, her hands gripped the strap of her bag, just as Valyn had seen her do countless times before. The image caused a smile to bubble up on her lips. Asta just looked more confused, but Valyn did not care. She would weather anything, so long as Asta was there.

After a few minutes of silence, Asta's voice broke it, and it was the single loveliest thing Valyn had ever heard. "Do… Do I know you, my lady?"

Valyn kept smiling as she replied, "Valyn is my name."

Asta's eyebrows knit together, and she said the name as if it were a forgotten taste. "Valyn?"

The woman nodded. "There was a word I said to you once, though I neglected to tell you its meaning."

Asta shook her head. "I'm sorry, I am... I have the strangest feeling..."

"Would you like to hear it?"

The girl's lips parted very slowly, her words careful. "Somehow, Lady Valyn, I feel as though I should."

Valyn's eyes locked onto Asta's as she said, "*Asavakkit.*"

Asta took a step forward. Her face worked through a whirlwind of emotions, but when she focused on Valyn, there was the smallest, most wonderful spark. They both took another step towards each other, until they were just an arm's length away. Valyn did not reach out, though she ached to do so. Asta's knuckles were white as she gripped her bag tighter, but she looked up at the other elf with the ghost of a smile on her lips.

"Forgive me, but I seem to have a memory of you I know not the origin of. But..." Asta paused. "You were supposed to tell me what that word meant when I returned."

Valyn nodded, gesturing to the lake. "I know. Come sit with me, and perhaps I'll tell you."

Asta smiled—a true, radiant smile—and Valyn knew there was nothing in the world as perfect as that sight.

They sat down together at the edge of the lake, Asta's blue-eyed gaze softening with every word they exchanged, and Valyn made peace with whatever came next. As long as Asta was alive and well, Valyn had purpose, and loneliness would never plague her again.

The End

From the author:

Thank you so much for picking up this novella!

This is only my second book, and it all started from one single scene idea that ended up being Chapter 13.

I listen to a lot of Kikuo, and *Hole-dwelling* is my favorite song.
Whenever I heard it, I always thought of it as this flowing dance, but with something darker happening at the same time.

We dance. We spin around. Our dance is a queer one
We thought we were dancing
We thought we were laughing
We thought we were falling over
We thought we were screaming

And so, *Golden Blade, Silver Veins* was born.

As always, I want to thank my editor for doing what he does, and everyone else that read my screen-filling messages about this story. It was originally going in a very different direction, but I'm so happy with where it ended up, like a journey with welcome detours.

So thank you again dear readers, it means the world to have others spend their time reading my work, and I will continue to create stories for as long as I possibly can.

Magnus October